DEATH'S SHADOW

SALLY RIGBY

This is a work of fiction. Names, characters, business, events and incidents are the products of the author's imagination. Any resemblance to actual persons, living or dead, or actual events is purely coincidental.

Copyright © Sally Rigby, 2024

The moral right of the author has been asserted.

All rights reserved. No part of this book may be reproduced or used in any manner without the prior written permission of the copyright owner.

To request permissions, contact the publisher at rights@stormpublishing.co

Ebook ISBN: 978-1-80508-590-4
Paperback ISBN: 978-1-80508-591-1

Previously published in 2024 by Top Drawer Press.

Cover design: Stuart Bache Design
Cover images: Shutterstock

Published by Storm Publishing.
For further information, visit:
www.stormpublishing.co

ALSO BY SALLY RIGBY

Cavendish & Walker Series

Deadly Games

Fatal Justice

Death Track

Lethal Secret

Last Breath

Final Verdict

Ritual Demise

Mortal Remains

Silent Graves

Kill Shot

Dark Secrets

Broken Screams

Buried Fear

A Cornwall Murder Mystery

The Lost Girls of Penzance

The Hidden Graves of St Ives

Murder at Land's End

Detective Sebastian Clifford Series

Web of Lies

Speak No Evil

Never Too Late

Hidden From Sight
Fear the Truth
Wake the Past

To instantly receive the free novella, *The Night Shift*, featuring Whitney when she was a Detective Sergeant, ten years ago, sign up for Sally Rigby's free author newsletter:

www.sallyrigby.com/night

ONE

Monday

Detective Chief Inspector Whitney Walker paced the floor and glanced at her watch for the tenth time. Where on earth was George? It wasn't like her to be late. If anything, she was obsessive about good timekeeping.

Whitney's thoughts turned to when she'd first met the forensic psychologist and university lecturer, Dr Georgina Cavendish. Against her better judgement, Whitney had agreed to her assisting them in a case involving some student murders. It turned out to be the best thing that could have happened and they'd been solving cases together since.

If anyone had told Whitney at the time that she'd not only end up being best friends with the uptight, socially awkward woman, but she'd also be her bridesmaid, she'd have laughed in their faces. But she couldn't have been more wrong.

It had been a year since Ross's proposal, and the wedding was in thirteen days' time.

Several times over the last twelve months Whitney had wondered whether George might back out. Not because her friend didn't love Ross. She did and they were great together, although total opposites. It was more the whole family and wedding thing that wasn't on George's radar.

'I'm really sorry, I don't know where George is,' Whitney said, turning to Sheila Faulkner, the seamstress, who was standing by a rail of wedding dresses tapping her foot impatiently, waiting to do last-minute alterations to the wedding gown and bridesmaid dress.

'I have another appointment straight after this,' the woman said. 'If she doesn't arrive soon, then we'll have to rearrange.'

'The wedding's a week on Saturday – we really don't have time to do that. I'm sure she'll be here soon. Give her a few more minutes, please. I'm sorry,' Whitney said, repeating her apology in the hope the dour woman would cut them some slack. It wasn't like they'd let her down in the past.

Whitney had been totally bowled over when George had asked her to be the only bridesmaid. She knew she'd be invited to attend the wedding – George had promised her that – but this was such an honour. George had suggested that Whitney's two-year-old granddaughter, Ava, should be a flower girl, but after giving it some thought they decided against it. The child was going through a decidedly wild stage at the moment and there was no guaranteeing that she'd stay still and not charge around all over the place.

The wedding was being held at the gorgeous manor house that George and Ross had bought last year, with a marquee in the garden. Her friend had really wanted a small wedding but Ross had a large family, and despite careful planning, they were still expecting over a hundred guests. Their families were very different, and Whitney couldn't wait to see how it all panned out. It would certainly be interesting from a sociological point of view.

When she'd mentioned that to George, her friend had dismissed it, saying that she had no interest in worrying about something she couldn't control and that they'd all have to deal with it themselves. Very typical George. Always keeping her emotions in check. Except for the one time when she'd split with Ross after he'd proposed the first time. That had actually taken a toll on her, and everyone was pleased when they got back together.

'Well, that's as may be,' Sheila said, interrupting Whitney's reminiscences, 'but I've still got the next bride coming in, and we've got to get this sorted.'

'Why don't we start with mine?' Whitney suggested. 'I'll go and try it on.'

'Hmmm. I suppose so. But I'll still need sign-off from the bride,' the woman said, scowling.

Whitney had never warmed to Sheila, but she was the best, and George was very happy with her designs. With George being so tall and Whitney being short, off-the-peg wasn't an option.

The door opened, and Whitney turned sharply, her eyes lighting up. 'At last. You're here,' she said, clasping her hands together as George strode purposefully into the shop.

'Apologies for being late,' George said with a small nod, meeting Whitney's eager gaze and then the dressmaker's more impatient one.

Sheila checked her watch, lips pursed. 'You're cutting it very fine,' she said crisply. 'I have another appointment shortly.'

Whitney tipped her head, brow furrowed. 'I'm sure you had a good reason. What was it? The traffic?'

George shook her head. 'No, actually it wasn't. I've been at a criminology conference all day, and one of the presenters died unexpectedly.' She met their eyes. 'I was about to leave when one of the conference organisers approached me. They'd like me to take his place on the Wednesday-afternoon panel.'

Whitney arched an eyebrow in surprise. 'That's short notice.'

'It's okay. There's no need for any preparation. It's on serial killers,' George replied, waving a dismissive hand.

'Well, you are an expert in that field.' Whitney grinned, turning to look at Sheila, whose eyes were wide. She was sorely tempted to leave it at that, to see how the dressmaker reacted, but they didn't have the time. 'It's okay, Sheila. There's nothing to worry about. I'm a police officer, and George here, aka renowned forensic psychologist Dr Cavendish, helps my team on our more serious cases.'

Sheila expelled a loud breath, clearly relieved. 'Okay, but we still need to get a move on. Your dresses are hanging up.'

Whitney and George hurried over to the joint fitting room and started stripping off.

'What happened to the dead guy?' Whitney asked, glancing over at George whilst gingerly stepping into her dress and wiggling herself into it.

'Jonathan Hargrove,' George said, removing her dress from the hanger. 'All I know is that he was found in his room after lunch and it's a suspected heart attack. The conference is being held at Linwood Conference Centre.'

'Oh, I know the place.' Whitney nodded. 'It's meant to be lovely there. Set in a country house with beautiful grounds, I believe.'

'Yes, that's right. Not that I've had time to look round the garden.' George sighed. 'The main conference only started today, although there was a preconference day yesterday, and Hargrove did a presentation on his Death's Shadow theory then.'

Whitney's eyes widened. 'Death's Shadow? Yikes – sounds creepy.'

'It's an alternative view on what makes a serial killer. Controversial in many circles.'

'Oh... interesting. Did you attend?'

George shook her head. 'No, I was busy with Ross sorting

out seating arrangements. I can't see what the problem is. People should sit where's most convenient to us.'

Whitney smirked knowingly. 'Don't tell me, Ross pays more attention to who gets on with whom and tries to accommodate that. Am I right?'

'Yes, but it's ridiculous,' George huffed, throwing up a hand.

'Of course it is.' Whitney rolled her eyes. 'So you had to miss this presentation on serial killers because of it?'

'It didn't matter. I'm familiar with his theory. There would have been further discussion on it over the conference. But now he's dead, I'm unsure whether that will happen.'

'How many people are attending?'

'I believe there are a hundred and twenty delegates. We've had more in the past. This is the first time it's been held in Lenchester – the university's sponsoring it.'

'Your department?'

'No. Criminology. Although many of my colleagues will be attending some, if not all, of the lectures.'

'And you?'

'I'll attend some presentations, but we'll save this conversation for later,' George said, her eyes focused intently on Whitney. She gave an approving nod. 'Sheila will be getting impatient. I'm very pleased with the way your dress has turned out.'

Whitney turned to the full-length mirror, her fingers gliding over the sleek fabric of the bridesmaid's dress. It was a classy, close-fitting azure dress with a deep V-neckline that complemented Whitney's dark curls and eyes. The dress flared out subtly at the hips and reached her ankles. Whitney was relieved that George hadn't wanted fussy dresses – on Whitney's tiny frame, too many ruffles would've made her look like a pastel marshmallow.

'Thank you, I really like it.' Whitney smiled, adjusting the cap sleeves. 'I think it's a lovely design, simple but elegant.

Although I don't know what you're going to do with my hair.' She ran her fingers self-consciously through her mass of wild curls.

'I think you should wear it down,' George said decisively. 'We'll have small flowers throughout to complement the dress.'

Whitney laughed. 'Well, it's your wedding. If you want this mess of frizz, go for it.' She cocked her head. 'By the way, you look absolutely stunning.'

George was resplendent in an ivory gown that skimmed her tall, lean frame. Tiny pearl buttons ran down the front from the bateau neckline to the waist. The short, puffed sleeves and nipped-in bodice showcased George's striking silhouette.

'Yes, I'm very happy with it,' George murmured, smoothing the skirt.

'Ross is going to lose his mind when he sees you.' Whitney grinned. 'You look fantastic.'

George glanced at her reflection approvingly. 'It doesn't appear to need any alterations. We'll see if Sheila agrees.'

They left the fitting room and headed into the main shop. 'Finally. I could hear you chatting. You first on the plinth, Whitney,' the woman ordered.

Whitney stood and Sheila walked around pulling at the sides. 'This fits well. Thank goodness you didn't go on a pre-wedding crash diet, like so many brides and bridesmaids do. All that needs fixing is the hem. Do you have the shoes you're going to be wearing with you?'

Whitney looked at George. 'Oops, I forgot them,' she said. 'Did you bring yours?'

'No, but we're both wearing two-inch heels,' George said, turning to Sheila.

'Okay, try these.' Sheila picked up a pair of shoes from a shelf behind her and handed them to Whitney, who slipped them on.

'Thanks.'

'This is the final fitting. The dress will be ready for collection in a week's time,' Sheila said as she finished adjusting Whitney's dress. 'You can get changed now. George, step up here.'

Whitney hurried back to the fitting room, leaving George standing tall on the plinth. As she whooshed the curtain behind her, her phone shrilled loudly. She grabbed it from her bag, glancing at the screen. Dr Claire Dexter. What did she want? The terse pathologist never called for a chat.

'Whitney speaking,' she answered briskly.

'I've got a suspicious death,' Claire said, without preamble. Pleasantries weren't Claire's strong suit.

'And you want me over now?' she asked, eyeing her watch. It was nearly five already.

'No, I have some more tests to do before coming to a final conclusion.'

Whitney's brows knitted. 'So why are you calling?'

'To give you warning. I'd have thought you'd be pleased to know in advance.'

Whitney bit back a sharp retort. Claire wasn't usually so forthcoming; she didn't want to jeopardise that ever happening again.

'I really appreciate it. Thanks, Claire. What can you tell me about the victim?'

'He was found at Linwood Conference Centre.'

'Oh,' Whitney exclaimed. 'Do you mean the suspected heart attack?'

'How do you know?' Claire asked brusquely.

'I'm with George having final dress fittings for the wedding. She was at the conference when it happened.'

'What does she know about it?' Claire asked.

'Nothing other than it was a suspected heart attack. What makes you believe it's a suspicious death?'

'No time for specifics now. Be at the morgue tomorrow morning, by which time I'll have confirmation.'

Claire ended the call without even saying goodbye. Again, no different from usual.

Whitney hurried out of the changing room into the shop, where George was talking to Sheila.

'Sorry to interrupt. Have we finished?' Whitney asked.

'Yes. Why?' George responded.

'Something's come up and I need a quick word with you.' Grabbing George's arm, Whitney pulled her friend into the fitting room.

'What is it?' George pulled herself from Whitney's grasp.

'I've had a call from Claire. She thinks we've got a suspicious death to investigate and you'll never guess who the victim is.'

'How am I expected to know?' George frowned as she slipped off the dress and replaced it on the hanger.

Whitney sighed. 'Because we were talking about him a moment ago. It's the man who died at the conference.'

'Jonathan Hargrove? I was informed by the conference organiser that it was a heart attack,' George said, appearing surprised at the news.

'Well, according to Claire it might not be. She's doing more tests and will let us know. I think we should head to the conference centre now to check things out. Do you have time?'

'Yes, but there's not much we can do until we have confirmation.'

'I know, but if Claire's right, then taking a look now will give us a head start.'

'Okay, I'll let Ross know I'm going to be late.'

'Where was he found?'

'In his bedroom, I believe.'

'Right, let's head there now.'

TWO

Monday

Whitney parked her car on the gravel drive of the conference centre and waited until George drew up behind her before getting out. She shivered as a gust of wind whistled past.

'Wow, this is lovely. I've always wondered what it looked like inside. I remember when they bought the house, it was totally run down. But look at it now.' Whitney gestured to the old Victorian manor house and the beautifully manicured grounds.

'Yes, it's very nice. I've attended several conferences here. They always do an excellent job,' George said.

'As you're familiar with the place, I'll let you lead the way.'

Whitney locked her car, although she was tempted not to in case someone wanted to steal it. She'd had the car for years and every time she'd planned on changing it something cropped up. Like the time Tiffany announced she was pregnant. That had changed everything. Babies weren't cheap, nor was turning the spare room into a nursery. Not that Whitney begrudged a penny of the expense.

Now that Ava was a little older, Tiffany was considering returning to university to finish off her engineering degree. They had a good crèche there, which she could use. Whitney was all for it. She'd managed a career as a young single mum, and knew that her daughter could do the same. In fact, Tiffany would probably make a better job of it. Tiffany never ceased to amaze her with how good she turned out to be, both as a mother and as a human being. Actually, Martin often commented on how proud he was of his daughter.

Whitney swallowed hard. Now wasn't the time to think about Martin. When he'd proposed, over a year ago, she'd initially said no, and then agreed to go on holiday with him, after one of their cases finished, to think things over. It hadn't worked out, and now he was working in Canada for a year and they were taking a break. Whitney would always be in contact with Martin, because he was Tiffany's father, and she loved him... but more as a friend, nothing else.

'Come on, let's go inside,' George said, cutting across her thoughts.

They headed through the main entrance, and up to the reception desk.

'Good evening, Dr Cavendish. I thought you'd gone for the day,' the young man behind the desk said.

'I'm back on another matter,' George confirmed.

Whitney held out her warrant card. 'I'm from Lenchester CID. I understand one of the conference attendees, Jonathan Hargrove, was found dead in his room earlier today.'

'Yes, that's right.' The man grimaced. 'It was awful. I was on duty and had to call the ambulance.'

'Has his room been cleaned?' Whitney asked, hoping it hadn't.

'No, the cleaners aren't in until tomorrow morning.'

'Good. I want you to hold off cleaning it. It should remain exactly as it was at the time of death,' Whitney said firmly, standing tall with her shoulders back, making it clear this was not a request.

'Why?' the man asked, his brow furrowing in confusion.

'When someone dies away from home, we take a closer look, as per standard procedure,' Whitney explained patiently. 'Please may I have a key to his room?'

The man's eyes flicked to the computer screen. 'Room 216 on the second floor. I'll give you a key card.'

Whitney inwardly grimaced as the card was prepared. She hated those things – they never worked properly for her.

'Thanks,' she said briskly as he passed the card over. 'I'll hang on to this, so don't change the code until we're done.'

The man nodded. 'I'll make a note of your request. My shift ends at eight.'

'Is reception open twenty-four hours?' George asked.

'No, we close at eight and don't offer room service.'

'Good to know,' Whitney said, making a mental note. 'We're heading to the room now, but will be back with more questions. Don't leave until we return.'

Panic crossed his face, as he stared at her. 'How long do you think you'll be? I have plans after work...'

Whitney held his gaze. 'We'll be as long as required,' she said firmly.

He flushed slightly under her steely look and mumbled his agreement.

They headed away from the reception towards the stairwell, ignoring the lifts. Whitney opted to take the stairs, determined to work in some extra exercise. She wanted to look her absolute best in the fitted bridesmaid's dress. Sheila had a point about wanting to diet for a wedding. Not that Whitney needed to lose any weight, but she wouldn't mind firming up a bit. The dress was fitted in such a way that it left no room to hide what could be called her 'problem' area.

Puffing slightly as they reached the second-floor landing,

Whitney shot a look at George, who seemed unfazed by the climb.

'Look at you – not even slightly out of breath.' Whitney gave a sigh. 'How'd you manage that?'

George shrugged. 'As you know, I work out regularly. A few flights of stairs don't pose an issue for me.'

They headed along the plush carpeted hallway, scanning door numbers, before finally reaching 216. Whitney slid the key card firmly into the slot. Nothing. She grimaced, lips pursed. Of course it didn't work.

'See.' She glared at the innocuous red light blinking back at her mockingly. 'I told you these things hate me. Maybe I emit some kind of anti-technology force field.' She shoved the key in again, but to no avail.

George looked mildly amused. 'I sincerely doubt that's the issue.' She held out a hand. 'Here, allow me.'

Whitney reluctantly passed the card over. 'I warn you, it won't work any better for you.'

But as George smoothly swiped the card through, the light went green and the door clicked open obligingly.

'How...?' Whitney's mouth fell open indignantly. She stabbed an accusing finger at the door. 'Why does it hate me and not you?'

George's eyes crinkled in amusement. 'No idea. But we're in now, so let's focus on investigating this scene.'

Whitney pushed the door open wide and strode into the room, her gaze sweeping the surroundings. She pulled some disposable gloves from her pocket and tugged them on briskly before handing a pair to George.

'This is now a potential crime scene,' she declared. 'We need to treat it carefully.' She glanced over at George. 'We know the victim was found shortly after lunch, correct?'

George gave a single nod. 'Yes, I believe that's right.'

'Do we know who found him?' Whitney asked.

'Unfortunately not,' George replied, gloved hands folded in front of her. 'I don't have any further details.'

'We'll need to find out, if Hargrove's death proves suspicious,' Whitney murmured, prowling slowly around the room. It was a comfortable space – nice furnishings, tidy desk, a wide bed.

She gestured at the bed, brow furrowing. 'It looks like he was lying on the bed – look at the body imprint in the cover.' She glanced inquiringly at George. 'Was he found lying on the bed, do you know?'

George shrugged slightly. 'As I said, I wasn't given specifics on where or how he was discovered.'

'I know, just thinking aloud,' Whitney said apologetically. 'There's his laptop.' She picked it up from where it was stashed inside a case beside the bed, placed it on the duvet cover, and opened it. 'We'll take this with us.' She pulled out a large evidence bag and placed it inside. 'Have a look through the wardrobe, George. I'm going into the bathroom and see what's in there.'

She headed purposefully towards the small bathroom, scanning the space. Next to an electric toothbrush and tube of toothpaste by the sink was a toiletries bag. Inside were two small boxes of medication.

'Hey, George, do you know what amlodipine is for?' she called out.

'That's a blood pressure medication, I believe,' George's voice carried back.

Whitney examined the next bottle. 'Okay, and what about allopurinol?'

'That's used for gout if I'm not mistaken, but I'd need to check,' George answered.

Whitney took a photograph of the meds to show Claire when they visited the morgue, and returned them to where she'd found them in order for Forensics to check them. She headed back into the room.

'So, what we're saying is Jonathan Hargrove— Actually, come to think of it, how old is he?'

'I'm not certain, but I'd say he was in his fifties,' George replied, tossing a glance in Whitney's direction.

'Okay, so he's got high blood pressure and possibly gout. So, that means he must drink a lot of red wine and eat excessive amounts of red meat,' Whitney said.

'That's a common myth,' George said, giving a slight negative shake of her head. 'Whilst those factors can sometimes contribute, gout is actually a form of arthritis not caused solely by diet.'

'Oh, good to know. There's nothing that looks out of place in the bathroom. What about in the wardrobe? Anything of note?'

'No. There are two jackets hanging, and some casual clothes and underwear in the drawers. Nothing appears to have been disturbed. There's no sign of any scuffle or someone rummaging through Hargrove's possessions, so I would say nothing went on here,' George said.

Whitney raised a sceptical brow. 'Apart from the fact that he was found dead in the room. This room needs to be cordoned off. We'll leave it locked, and go back to reception. We need CCTV footage from around the area. I noticed some hallway cameras, so let's see if there are any near the lift as well. We need to know who was in the vicinity of the room prior to his death. And that's staff as well as conference attendees.'

'Good idea,' George said, pulling off her gloves.

Ensuring the door locked securely behind them, Whitney and George headed briskly back down the plush hallway.

Whitney gestured upwards at a dome camera overlooking the corridor. 'See there? That one covers the whole hall.'

As they waited for the lift, she noticed another high on the wall. 'And another camera pointing this way. At least they have decent security coverage here.'

George gave a slight nod as the doors opened. 'Well, it is a newly refurbished centre that hosts frequent conferences.'

'Do they run multiple events at the same time?'

'Definitely. Currently there's a medical conference, a business conference, and the criminology conference,' George said.

The doors opened on the ground floor and they headed towards the reception.

Whitney marched up to the receptionist and fixed him with her police officer's stare. 'We've finished in the room for now, but no one's to go inside. I want a "No Entry" sign put on the door to make sure that no one from housekeeping, or other staff members, accidentally go in there.'

'Yes, okay. I can certainly arrange that.'

'I'll keep hold of this key card. I'd like to see some security camera footage showing the second-floor hall, lift area, and also in the main conference areas.'

The receptionist fidgeted and cleared his throat. 'I don't have the authority to release it. I'll have to ask the manager for permission.'

'Call them now,' Whitney said, trying not to sound irritated at the delay.

'She's actually popped out.'

'Do you have her number?'

'Yes.' The man nodded.

'Right, I suggest you give her a quick call. Explain that the police are here and they would like to see CCTV footage from the last twenty-four hours.'

'Yes, okay,' he muttered. He picked up the phone, dialled a number, and when it had been answered he explained the situation. He ended the call and looked directly at Whitney. 'My manager has given permission.'

'Here's my email address,' Whitney said, handing out her card. 'Send the footage straight away.'

They stepped away from the desk, leaving the receptionist to get on with the task.

'Have we finished here, now?' George asked.

'Not quite. Show me where the conference is being held, please.'

George nodded briskly. 'Follow me.'

They headed down the hall to a set of double doors. Pushing them open, George gestured at the large auditorium filled with rows of seats facing a stage.

'This is the main conference room. We start off together here, then break into smaller sessions throughout each day.'

Whitney walked along the aisle between seats, peering around. 'And where are the breakout rooms located?'

'Just off this auditorium,' George replied. 'There are four rooms accessible from side doors here to keep everything self-contained.'

Coming back up the aisle, Whitney asked, 'How many big auditorium spaces like this does the centre have?'

'You'd have to check with reception because I'm not sure.'

'Will do.' Whitney planted her hands on her hips. 'And this whole area is where your criminology gathering's happening?'

'Correct.'

'Where was Hargrove's lecture held yesterday?'

George spread her hands apologetically. 'I couldn't make it – table planning, remember? We could enquire at reception.'

'Oh yeah. Let's do that.'

Back at the front desk, Whitney waited somewhat impatiently, toe tapping, whilst the receptionist finished with another guest. When he finally turned to them, she asked crisply, 'Where was Professor Hargrove's Sunday lecture held?'

The man checked his computer. 'That was in Rosewood Two, one of the smaller breakouts.'

'And can you tell me how many people attended?'

'No. You'll have to speak to the conference organisers about that.'

Whitney sighed, glancing at her watch. 'Okay. How many conference rooms do you have here?'

'We have four large, each of which with their own breakouts. Plus, some smaller standalone rooms. We can comfortably accommodate up to four conferences simultaneously.'

'Thank you. Have you sent me the footage yet?'

'I'm getting to it,' he said. 'I'll need help from someone in IT. I'm about to phone them. I'll send it as soon as possible.'

'Thank you. We'll need it first thing tomorrow at the very latest.'

They strode out of reception and outside into the cool March air of the car park.

'Is there anything else you need?' George said. 'Because I really need to get home. We have wedding tasks to deal with.'

'No, that's all. We'll visit Claire at the morgue tomorrow morning.' Whitney paused a moment. 'Are you able to come with me?'

'I'd planned on attending the conference, but it's not imperative. What time do you wish to go?'

'Pick me up from the station at eight-thirty. We'll go in your car. You can drop me back off afterwards. If it's a suspicious death, are you able to work with me on the case?'

'Yes, I'm sure I can fit that in.'

'Will Ross mind?'

'No. It's a working day, so instead of being at the conference, I'll be with you. Or maybe I can combine the two, and attend any presentations that are of particular interest.'

'Right, I'll see you in the morning. Text me when you've arrived tomorrow morning and I'll come down to the car park. It will save you having to come inside.'

THREE

Tuesday

'My money's on a yellow polka-dot ankle-length skirt with an aquamarine lurex waistcoat and a puffy-sleeved bright blue blouse,' Whitney said as she slipped into the car the following morning and pulled her seat belt around her, clicking it in place. She grinned in George's direction.

George frowned. 'I'm afraid you'll have to be more explicit. I've no idea what you mean.'

She started the engine and drove towards the station car park entrance, to take them to the morgue for their meeting.

'For the wedding. You've invited Claire and Ralph, haven't you?' Whitney asked, tilting her head to one side.

'Yes, I have, as I believe we've already discussed.'

'Well, there you go then. I'm talking about what Claire's going to wear, which I'm betting is multicoloured, and totally clashing. Oh... I forgot the shoes. Hmm... silver slip-ons with a diamanté buckle on the front. Thoughts?'

'Oh, I see,' George said, letting out a sigh. She was in no mood to engage in supposition. Her head was full of all that needed doing before the wedding, which, much to her dismay, seemed to be taking over her entire life.

'You do know that she's not going to be dressed like anybody else, don't you?'

'I'm unsure how Claire's going to dress, apart from the fact that she does wear clothes that are a tad out-there, and I don't expect for my wedding it'll be any different,' George replied, refusing to be drawn into Whitney's fantasies.

Whitney burst out laughing. 'You do crack me up. You know exactly what Claire's like with her wardrobe, and she's not going to let us down for the wedding. I'll make sure to get some photos.'

'Why? What are you going to do with them? I hope you don't intend to put them up on social media to try to embarrass her.' George gave a stern glance in her friend's direction.

'George, what do you take me for? Of course not. It's for posterity, that's all. We love Claire and all her little foibles. Mind you, between your idiosyncrasies and Claire's, I'm not sure how I survive on a daily basis.'

George gave another sideways glare at her friend, who was shuffling in her seat as if unable to sit still. 'What's got into you this morning? You're full of jokes and not at all like your normal, verging-on-morose self at this time of day.'

'Well, it could be that I've already had two huge mugs of coffee because I got up early. Ava had a bad night and I couldn't go back to sleep after. But also, I'm really pleased because Tiffany's received notification that she can complete her course. That means she's back on track to be an engineer working on bridges.'

That combination explained why her friend was being so unusually hyperactive. George could forgive that.

'You do realise there aren't many bridges around here for her to work on. She may have to travel,' George said, wanting to ensure Whitney was aware of what Tiffany's success might entail.

Whitney pouted. 'George, stop putting a dampener on it. I just want her to finish off her education and make a career for herself. And of course I know there's a distinct lack of bridges here in Lenchester. Anyway, back to Claire. Are you going to take my bet?'

'I wasn't aware that we'd made one.'

'You drive me insane,' Whitney said. 'Anyway, what do you think she'll be wearing today?'

'Whitney, I'm not going to engage in a "Guess Claire's Outfit" game because from past experience, we're unlikely to be correct.'

'Fair enough. In that case, change of topic. Let's talk about the wedding preparations. How are they going?'

'Dietary requirements continue to plague me although, thankfully, the caterer is on top of it – providing no one else comes along with another allergy for us to consider. And, as I mentioned yesterday, we've been putting the final touches on the seating plan, which we managed to finish last night. Thank goodness.'

'Where am I sitting?'

'You're on a table with Tiffany and Ava, Claire and Ralph, and two of Ross's friends from university with their partners.'

'I don't know them.'

'You soon will. They're most agreeable.'

'Good. I'm looking forward to it. If they're anything like Ross, they'll be good company.'

They drove in silence for the remainder of the journey, George having to force her mind on the road and not on the work piling up back at her office because of everything else on her mind.

'We're here,' George said as they pulled into the hospital car park and came to a halt near the morgue entrance.

The moment they entered the building, they were hit by the unique smell.

Whitney wrinkled her nose. 'You know, it seems ages since we've been here. I can't remember the last suspicious death or murder that we've had. I've almost missed our regular visits. Apart from the stink, obviously.'

'Well, it's not something I enjoy, but you'd get used to it if this was your workplace. Did Claire specify a time for us to arrive?'

'No, she just told me to call in. You know what Claire's like – whenever we arrive, it won't be convenient.'

They pushed open the double doors leading to the morgue and walked into the vast space. Claire was sitting at her desk in the office off to the side. She turned as the door banged behind them.

'Ah, good. You're here. I have a nightmare of a day ahead of me and could do without any interruptions,' the pathologist said, tossing a glance in their direction.

'Morning, Claire. Nice to see you, too,' Whitney said, with a grin.

'Come on then.' Claire stood up and reached for her white lab coat.

From out the corner of her eye, George noticed Whitney smirking. Claire was wearing a pair of bright pink Wellington boots with some ribbed purple tights, over which she had a grey pinafore dress and a green checked shirt underneath. Although George wasn't quite as obsessed with Claire's attire as Whitney, it was certainly puzzling how she managed to put her clothes together in such a distinctive style. Whitney had once tried to find out exactly where Claire shopped, but to no avail. The pathologist wasn't prepared to give up that secret.

'Follow me,' Claire said slipping her arms into her lab coat.

They followed her into the centre of the room where, on the stainless-steel table, lay Jonathan Hargrove. His body was pale under the harsh light. The red stitched lines in the shape of a V on his body where Claire had made her incisions were vivid against his pale skin. Whitney stepped closer to Claire and scrutinised the body. George held back for a second, making sure there was no blood that might take her unawares.

It wasn't that she couldn't handle seeing blood now. She'd undergone sufficient hypnotherapy sessions to make it bearable – although not to the extent that she could return to the medical profession like the rest of her family. Blood aversion did that to a person. That didn't matter, though. She loved being a forensic psychologist and certainly didn't feel she'd settled for second best. Certain members of her family didn't view it in the same way, though.

'Are you still thinking this is a suspicious death?' Whitney said, cutting into George's thoughts and focusing her attention back on the body on the table.

'Yes, I am,' Claire replied. 'There was a large amount of insulin in his body – sufficient to have mimicked the symptoms of a heart attack.'

'We looked around his bedroom and the only medications we found were for blood pressure and gout. Certainly no insulin there.'

Whitney pulled out her phone and showed Claire a photo of the meds.

'What alerted you to this not being a normal heart attack?' George asked, peering at the lifeless body on the table.

'The initial blood test showed the victim had a very low blood sugar level and I inspected further. I found an injection site in his lower back.'

'But doesn't everyone have insulin in their body? How are you able to ascertain that the death was down to insulin poisoning?' George asked.

'Well, to put it simply, yes, insulin is a naturally occurring hormone. It's not always easy to differentiate between natural insulin and injected insulin. Insulin on its own is difficult to trace, but its precursor, C-peptide, isn't in insulin that's directly injected into the body. It's normally produced naturally by the pancreas.'

'I'm not sure I understand,' Whitney said, frowning.

Claire gave a frustrated sigh. 'Right. In laymen's terms: Hargrove had a lack of C-peptide in his blood. Because that was combined with a low blood sugar level and raised insulin, it led me to conclude this was a suspicious death, and the victim was given insulin. This is why I began looking for an injection site and found one in the back. Is that simple enough for you, Whitney? I'd have thought better of you.'

'Thank you, Claire. I get it now. I didn't get much sleep last night, so I'm not firing on all cylinders. Not to mention the overload of caffeine this morning.' Whitney gave a tiny shrug.

'Whatever,' Claire muttered, rolling her eyes.

'How can someone stab him with a syringe full of insulin without him trying to stop them? There was no signs of any struggle in his room. Any thoughts?' Confusion flickered across Whitney's face.

'How many times do I have to tell you that those conversations are for you and your team and not me?' Claire said, tutting loudly.

'Could it have been suicide?' Whitney mused.

'Theoretically, yes,' Claire replied. 'But that would have required a degree of flexibility that most people don't have.'

'True. And if it was suicide, then surely he would have injected himself in the thigh, or some other easy to reach place. Would he have died straight away after being injected?'

'With sufficient insulin, there would have been an immediate impact on the blood sugar level, reducing it to fatal levels. It would have led to a hypoglycaemic shock.'

'Apart from the body being brought here, was he moved post-mortem?' George asked.

'No,' Claire said.

'Okay,' Whitney said. 'Let's pull this all together. Hargrove was murdered with an overdose of insulin, and because of the immediate effect, it would have happened in his room. He would have either fallen onto the bed, or lain down of his own volition. Claire, would that fit in with your findings?'

'Yes. The speed with which the insulin would have taken effect would mean that he was injected close to where he was found.'

'Why choose insulin as a murder weapon?' Whitney mused.

'Maybe the killer had access to it, if they're diabetic?' George suggested. 'Or they intended it to look like a heart attack. Especially if the person wasn't aware that all unexpected deaths in a public place are brought here to the morgue. If it had happened in Hargrove's home it would have been a different story.'

'I agree,' said Claire. 'It would have most likely been classified as a heart attack.'

'Do you have a time of death?' Whitney asked.

'Between eleven a.m. and two p.m. yesterday.'

'Which takes us over the lunchtime period and fits in with what we already know. That he was seen after morning lectures and was found in his room later,' George said.

'Agreed,' Whitney said, nodding.

'Okay. Your time's up,' Claire said, waving her hand as if dismissing them from the area. 'I'm expecting two bodies from a nasty crash that happened earlier on the M1.'

'No problem. We're going,' Whitney said. 'By the way, was anything found on his person?'

'His phone. It's over there, bagged up.' Claire nodded towards a table on the far side of the room.

'Excellent. We need to speak to his next-of-kin. I'm assuming they've already been informed.'

'Yes, his wife identified the body yesterday afternoon.'

'We'll have to let her know the latest findings,' Whitney said with a sigh. 'Thanks, Claire.'

As they went to leave, Whitney stopped and turned back. 'Claire, what are you wearing for George's wedding?'

The pathologist glanced up from covering Hargrove's body with a sheet, and gave a half-smile. 'It's going to be a surprise. But I'm very pleased with what I found. Go. I'm busy. We may or may not see each other before the twenty-third.'

Once they'd left the morgue, Whitney turned to George. 'I knew it. She's going to be dressed in something crazy. I told you.'

'Don't be ridiculous, Whitney. Now, what are you intending for us to do next?'

'We'll go to the station first, and then see Mrs Hargrove. From there, we'll head to the conference centre. You're free to be with me all day, I hope?'

'Yes. The panel that I'm on in place of Hargrove isn't until tomorrow. Anyway, this takes precedence.'

FOUR

Tuesday

'Listen up, everyone. I want your full attention,' Whitney said when she and George entered the incident room at Lenchester CID. She glanced around at her officers and was silent for a few seconds until all eyes were focused on her. 'We have a suspicious death, according to Dr Dexter. We've just arrived back from the morgue.'

'I thought it was too good to be true,' ex-Detective Constable Frank Taylor called out. 'It's been months since we've had a murder. Although I suppose we should be grateful – we don't want to lose our reputation for being the murder capital of the world. Does this mean late shifts?'

'First of all, I'd hardly call our murder rate the worst in the world,' DC Doug Baines said. 'And as for having to work late, it's not your problem now you're a civilian. You can come and go as you please. You don't have to do the long hours that we do.'

Frank had officially retired earlier in the year but Whitney had convinced him to stay on as a civilian worker. Although he tended to be lazy unless pushed, he was a loyal and trustworthy member of the team. Whitney couldn't imagine them working without him. Luckily, he'd agreed – although she suspected it was with encouragement from his wife, who'd confided in Whitney at his retirement party that she wasn't looking forward to him being under her feet all day.

'Actually, that's not true. In my contract, I'm expected to work longer hours if necessary. Anyway, what's it to you?'

'Look at you, getting all assertive in your old age.' Doug grinned.

'Will you two please stop?' Whitney said. 'Frank's right. Just because he's now a civilian doesn't mean he has any less responsibility than you, as we're all aware.'

'Then what's the point of it?' Doug said.

'You know full well what it is. He's retired on his pension, and now he's come back to work. And I, for one, am glad that you're here, Frank. Although, God help me if you two carry on with your constant bickering. Do you know I actually dream about it sometimes?'

'Do you?' Frank said, puffing out his chest.

'Oh, for goodness' sake, stop it,' Doug said.

'Right. Enough with the *banter*.' Whitney did air quotes with her fingers. 'There's been a suspicious death – a Professor Jonathan Hargrove.' Whitney took a pen from the whiteboard and wrote the name. 'He's a criminologist. Actually, George, you can tell us about him.'

George stepped forward. 'I've been attending an international criminology conference where he was one of the speakers. Jonathan Hargrove was a maverick, or certainly considered to be one in certain circles. He'd come up with a controversial theory, which he'd named Death's Shadow, on what makes a serial killer. He'd been presenting his theory at various conferences recently, and on Sunday, the day before the conference officially began, he gave an early presentation. He was due to be on a panel tomorrow, but I've been asked to take his place.'

'Thanks, George. We need to get started. First of all, Ellie, I'd like you to do a thorough background check into Jonathan Hargrove.' Whitney glanced across at the young detective constable who was sitting at her desk. She appeared to be staring in the right direction, but judging by her facial expression, her mind was elsewhere. 'Ellie,' Whitney called out sharply, sounding harsher than she'd intended.

The officer started, glanced up at Whitney, eyes wide, then proceeded to burst into floods of tears.

Crap. Whitney hadn't meant for that to happen. Ellie had never done that before.

Whitney rushed over, guilt coursing through her veins. 'What's the matter?' she asked quietly.

'It's nothing,' Ellie said, sniffing, shaking her head.

'Come into my office.' Whitney guided the young woman from her seat and looked over her shoulder at the other team members, who all looked as shocked as Whitney was feeling. 'We'll be back in a minute.'

She led Ellie into her office, and they sat down at the coffee table. 'I'm sorry for snapping. I didn't mean it.'

'It's not that, guv. It's...' Her voice trailed off.

'What is it? Has something happened? You know you can tell me.' Whitney rested her hand on the officer's arm.

'Dean dumped me,' Ellie said, bursting into tears again.

Whitney reached for the box of tissues in the centre of the coffee table and held it out for Ellie, who took one and wiped her eyes. 'Oh no. I'm really sorry. Is it permanent?'

Ellie nodded. 'Yes. He's met someone else. A nurse that he works with.' Ellie sniffed.

Whitney tensed. Ellie was like another daughter and she'd do anything to prevent her from getting hurt.

'Would you like to go home? Take some time until you feel like working?'

They needed her skills, but Whitney knew better than most how hard it was to concentrate on work when your mind was elsewhere.

'Thanks, but no,' Ellie said, shaking her head. 'All I'll do at home is get more upset. I didn't mean to break down in there. When you shouted at me, I jumped because I wasn't concentrating.'

'I didn't even mean to shout – it just came out. Sorry. The others are going to be wondering what's the matter. Have you told anyone?'

'No.' She sniffed.

'Would you like me to?'

'Yes, please. If I do, then I'll only start crying again,' Ellie said, giving a watery smile.

'How much detail shall I go into?' Whitney asked, not wanting to divulge too much if Ellie didn't want her to.

'You can tell them everything.'

'No problem. Why don't you go to the loo, wash your face and take a few deep breaths until you feel calmer? The rest of them will be very understanding. I've never worked with as close a team as this one.'

'Thanks,' Ellie said, standing. 'I'll go this way.' She headed out of the other door in Whitney's office, which meant avoiding coming face to face with the rest of the team.

Whitney returned to the incident room, and the chatting stopped immediately. They all stared in her direction, worried expressions on their faces.

'Okay, everyone, we've got to treat Ellie gently. The reason she's so upset is because Dean's split up with her. He's gone off with another woman.' Whitney sighed.

'Bastard,' Frank exploded, anger etched on his face. 'Just let me get hold of him and he'll know it.'

'That's enough, Frank,' DS Brian Chapman said, waving his arm in a placatory manner. 'We don't need that. Ellie needs our support, not our anger.'

'I know that, but all I'm saying is if I see him, he'll have me to answer to, and that's final.'

The door opened, and Ellie walked in.

'Ellie, we're all really sorry to hear what's happened,' DC Meena Singh said.

'Don't you worry. We're here for you,' Frank said. 'And if you want us to sort him out you only have to say because—'

'Frank,' Whitney warned.

'It's okay,' Ellie said, her voice cracking and a faint smile crossing her face. 'I appreciate your offer, but I want nothing to do with him from now on. It's over and that's that.'

'Well, the offer's there, anytime,' Frank said, who then glanced across at Whitney. 'Sorry, guv, but it had to be said. And now I'll be quiet.' He zipped his mouth shut.

Whitney smiled. 'Thanks, Frank. Right, let's get on. Ellie, I'd like you to look into Jonathan Hargrove. We brought his laptop back with us when we searched his room yesterday, before we had confirmation that it was a suspicious death. It's been sent to Forensics so, hopefully, Mac will get back to us pronto. But keep an eye on that. Brian, I'd like you to go through his mobile. It's here.' She walked over and handed it to him.

'What's happening now with the conference?' Brian asked, taking the phone from her. 'Are we going to stop it?'

'No, I don't believe that's a good idea. We don't want to alarm the delegates. If the murderer is one of them, they're most likely still there, believing that they've got away with it. It's our opinion that they intended for the death to appear to be from natural causes and hadn't factored in that the body would automatically have gone to the morgue and that Dr Dexter would have completed an investigation.'

'And nothing gets past her.'

'Absolutely,' Whitney agreed. 'A lesser qualified pathologist might well have missed it. I've had the CCTV footage sent over. Frank, I'd like you to go through that – I'll forward the link.'

'Okay, guv. Do you think we'll be working late tonight?' Frank asked.

'You're coming up with an excuse already?' Doug said, rolling his eyes.

'Actually, I don't mind staying. The wife's sister's coming round and all they want to do is chat and interrupt my telly viewing. I might as well be here, earning more money.'

'I don't envisage a late night but if that changes, you'll be the first to know,' Whitney said. 'Meena, please check the social media of Hargrove and anything relating to the conference.'

'Yes, guv,' the DC said.

'George and I will visit the victim's wife shortly to let her know the developments. As far as she's concerned, it was a natural death. She needs to be updated. The funeral will have to be postponed. Any questions?'

'Yes, please could you tell us more about this theory, Dr Cavendish?' Brian asked.

Whitney nodded. 'George, if you don't mind. It might help the investigation if we've all got more of a handle on what he was doing.'

'But not in academic speak, if you don't mind,' Doug said. 'Because you'll lose the lot of us.'

'Speak for yourself,' Frank piped up.

'I didn't realise you'd got your PhD. When was that?' Doug said.

'Boys, boys, boys...' Whitney said, holding up her hands. 'We don't have all day. George, please start, and I agree, keep it simple.'

George stepped forwards until she was facing the team. 'Hargrove's Death's Shadow theory proposes a somewhat radical idea about the psychology of serial killers. He believes serial killers aren't simply the result of a deviant personality, or mental illness, or a traumatic past – all theories that criminal psychologists have discussed and accepted for many years. Instead, Hargrove proposes that some individuals possess an innate, what he calls, "shadow self", which is a darker aspect of their psyche. This "self", when awakened under the right circumstances, compels them to kill. It's linked to Jungian theory, but I won't go into that now.'

'So, what he's saying is that it has nothing to do with their upbringing? It's already in them, but you can't tell?' Brian asked, frowning.

'That's correct. Hargrove believed that this shadow self can be present in anyone, not only those who demonstrate psychopathology – as in those factors we have linked in the past to being a serial killer. Basically, the shadow self stays dormant until it's triggered by specific environmental factors, like, say, extreme stress, personal loss, or societal pressures.'

'Do you believe this?' Frank asked.

'Well, it certainly challenges existing views in criminology, and it's caused a lot of controversy and debate. If it is proven, which it hasn't been to date, it would revolutionise the way we do criminal profiling and how we handle serial killers. But there are many critics of his theory.'

'It seems really complicated to me,' Frank said.

Doug opened his mouth to speak but Whitney jumped in, pre-empting whatever pithy retort the officer was about to say. 'No comment from you, Doug.'

'As if,' Doug said, smirking.

'I'm sorry if I've made it sound that way,' George said. 'It can be a difficult concept to comprehend.'

'Do you think that Hargrove could have been murdered by someone who took offence to his theory?' Doug asked.

'It's a possible line of enquiry but—' Whitney's phone rang, interrupting her. She pulled it out of her pocket and glanced at the screen; it was Claire. 'Hold on a moment. Let me take this. Whitney speaking.'

'Hargrove's medical records have finally come through. Some sort of computer glitch, which is why they've only just arrived,' the pathologist said with a sigh. 'He wasn't diabetic.'

'Thanks, Claire. That confirms our belief that he was murdered by someone with access to insulin.'

'Yes, it would seem so. Goodbye,' Claire said, ending the call.

Whitney returned the phone to her pocket. 'Okay, I'm sure you all heard that. Hargrove wasn't diabetic and hadn't accidentally overdosed on insulin.'

'Are we going to hold a press conference and announce the murder?' Brian asked.

'No, we're keeping this to ourselves – with the exception of Mrs Hargrove – and we'll ask her not to repeat it. After we've spoken to her, George and I will go to the conference to speak to the attendees. Questions?'

No one answered.

'Right, okay, good. Let's get on. I'd like to solve this one quickly because there's an important event coming up soon that I can't miss,' Whitney said, glancing at George, who rolled her eyes.

'Are you getting excited, Dr C?' Frank asked.

'There's no time for excitement, Frank. That's a wasted emotion when there's still so much to do before the event,' George said.

'Well, you asked, Frank,' Whitney said, laughing. 'You might think better of it next time, knowing George as we do.'

'I can't wait to see the photos,' Frank said.

'I'm not sure that there will be a photographer,' George said.

Whitney turned, her mouth open. 'What? You've got to have a photographer. For the memories. Does Ross know?'

'He's aware of my view and we discussed the possibility of

asking one of his family to take photos. It would make it more informal.'

'Surely your parents would want a proper photographer and a video of the occasion,' Whitney said, struggling to understand her friend's decision.

'It's not their wedding,' George said. 'And this isn't the time or place to talk about it. We have work to do.'

FIVE

Tuesday

'Have you met Jonathan Hargrove's wife before?' Whitney asked as they were driving towards the village in Warwickshire where the family lived.

'No, why would I?' George asked, tossing a glance in her direction and frowning.

'I thought you might've met at some academic function that she'd attended with him. According to Ellie's latest text, she doesn't work and he lectures in...' She paused and stared at her phone. '... Jungian and post-Jungian theories, dream analysis, and depth psychology. Whatever all that is.'

'That's why our paths haven't crossed. Yes, I know of him from his work in the psychology field, but he's not ventured into forensic psychology. I had heard about his latest theory because of the unease it was causing within academic circles. Did Ellie give you any more info on him?'

'He was fifty-five when he died. Had been married for twenty-eight years to Margot and has a twenty-six-year-old daughter. That's it,' Whitney said. She glanced down awkwardly. 'By the way, sorry about discussing your photographer in front of the others. I could see it made you uncomfortable.'

George waved a dismissive hand. 'It's not an issue and I wasn't put out by it. No need to apologise. It simply wasn't relevant at the time.'

Whitney fidgeted slightly. 'If you say so. Sorry, anyway. And for the record, I really think you should have one. It will be a lovely record to look back on when you're old and grey. If not for you, then for Ross and for your children if you have any.'

George's eyes widened in surprise; she turned her head sharply to look at Whitney. 'Why did you mention children?'

Whitney held her palms up innocently. 'No reason. Is it a problem?'

George pressed her lips together in a firm line, her brow furrowed. 'It's an issue that hasn't yet been resolved between us.'

Whitney leant in curiously, tilting her head. 'Don't you think you should, before the big day?'

George shook her head curtly, still not making eye contact. 'No. We've agreed to leave it until after.'

Whitney raised her eyebrows questioningly. 'I take it he wants kids and you don't?'

George sighed, turning back towards Whitney and met her gaze directly. 'It's not so straightforward. Yes, he would like children, but he's prepared to forego them, if I don't.'

Whitney nodded slowly as if taking in the complexity.

George focused on the road ahead. 'I haven't yet decided.'

Whitney touched George's arm lightly. 'Well, don't leave it too long – you're not getting any younger.'

George turned to meet her friend's expression. 'Yes, Whitney, I do realise that the chance of conceiving diminishes with age. But it's not a decision to be taken lightly.'

Whitney smiled warmly. 'I totally agree, but will say this.

Not a single day goes by when I don't think that having Tiffany was the best thing I ever did. And now we have Ava...' She paused, staring at George, who nodded.

'I do understand,' she said.

They were quiet for the rest of the journey, both seemingly deep in thought.

'It's very pretty out here,' Whitney said. 'Although it's probably a bit too remote for me. Doesn't look like there's even a village shop.'

'A lot of people enjoy living in a rural community,' George said, pulling into the driveway of the Hargroves' large, thatched cottage overlooking the village green, and parking behind a Mini Cooper.

'Oh, I've always fancied one of those,' Whitney said, pointing at it.

'You wouldn't like it. They're a bit tinny when you drive them,' George, a self-confessed petrol head, responded.

'Anything's got to be better than my car. I'll get around to changing it one day. When I don't have any other expenses.'

'Are you referring to Tiffany and Ava?' George asked.

'Not really. Well, yes, I suppose they do take up a good portion of my money. As a DCI, I'm not exactly underpaid, but the cost of everything these days, not to mention utilities, is crazy. You know, I said to Tiffany the other day that if it continues to go up, we'll have to have no heating and go to bed dressed in woolly hats, gloves and scarves.'

George stared at her friend. 'You know, if you ever need to borrow any money, I'm here.'

Whitney smiled. 'George, I'm a forty-year-old woman in a good job. I'm not going to borrow money from my friend. I can get by. I was exaggerating.' Whitney was touched by her friend's generosity, but no way would she ever consider taking a loan from her.

'Oh. I understand. Let's go inside.'

Whitney swallowed. This wasn't going to be easy. The woman was already grieving, let alone dumping the horror of her husband's murder on her doorstep. Whitney walked up to the door and rang the bell. After a couple of minutes, a man who looked to be in his sixties, dressed in jeans and casual shirt, answered. Whitney held out her identification.

'I'm Detective Chief Inspector Walker from Lenchester CID and this is Dr Cavendish. We're here to see Mrs Hargrove?'

'Come in.' He stepped to the side and gestured for them to enter.

'Who are you?' Whitney asked.

'I'm Ted Evans. A friend. I live in the next village.'

'How do you know Mrs Hargrove?' Whitney asked.

'We serve on the villages' joint parish council together.'

'I see. How is she doing?'

'Well, obviously devastated as one would expect.'

They followed him into a large hall and through to a square, traditionally furnished sitting room where a woman was sitting on one of the floral sofas.

Though she didn't appear particularly distressed.

'It's the police, Margot,' Evans said.

'Oh.'

The woman stood.

'No need to stand, Mrs Hargrove,' Whitney said. 'We're here to discuss Jonathan with you.'

Mrs Hargrove's face fell, but was that an act?

George would know.

Mrs Hargrove had seemed quite bright when they walked in, and now suddenly wore the look of a grieving widow.

'Please sit down. Would you like a coffee? Ted was about to make us one.'

'That would be lovely, thank you. Milk, no sugar for me.'

'The same for me,' George said.

Evans left them, and Mrs Hargrove gestured for them to sit on one of the sofas whilst she sat opposite. Between them was a low, dark mahogany coffee table with a coaster on each corner.

'We're very sorry for your loss,' Whitney said softly.

Mrs Hargrove dabbed at her eyes with a tissue she produced from her sleeve. 'Yes, it was awful. Jonathan was fine when he left for the conference, and then I learn that he had died.'

'So, it was very unexpected?' Whitney prodded.

'Yes, he didn't have any real health issues.' Mrs Hargrove shook her head.

'When did you last speak to him?'

'He left for the conference on Sunday morning.' The woman looked off into the distance.

'Didn't he phone you that evening?' Whitney asked, leaning forward.

Mrs Hargrove waved a hand. 'No, we didn't bother with constantly keeping in contact. We'd been together far too long for all that.'

Seriously? Whitney's mum and dad spoke every day throughout their marriage, wherever they might have been. Until her dad died.

'You've been married twenty-eight years, I believe?'

'Yes. We met at university. He was studying psychology and I was studying art history.' A faint smile crossed Mrs Hargrove's face.

'And you don't work at the moment?'

'No, I gave up work when we had our daughter. Once she'd left home, I busied myself with sitting on committees and doing charity work.'

Whitney shifted uncomfortably. 'We do have something to tell you, Mrs Hargrove, and this isn't going to be easy for you to hear.'

'What is it?' Mrs Hargrove said, taking hold of the gold chain around her neck and twisting it nervously in her fingers.

'An autopsy has been conducted on Jonathan's body, as you know, because it was an unexplained death away from home. The pathologist has confirmed his death to be suspicious.'

'Suspicious? What do you mean?' Mrs Hargrove's eyes widened.

'He died of an insulin overdose.'

Mrs Hargrove shook her head in disbelief. 'Insulin? He wasn't diabetic, so why would that happen?'

Whitney met her gaze. 'We don't believe it was accidental...'

Mrs Hargrove went pale, putting a hand to her mouth. 'Oh my goodness...' Her voice trailed off.

'Can you think of anyone who might have held a grudge against your husband?' Whitney asked.

'Um... he wasn't the easiest of men to get on with, and was very – how shall I put it? – self-centred. But that's what happens when you're married to a high-flying academic, I suppose. His life revolved around his work.'

The door opened, and Evans came in holding a tray of coffees.

'I'll leave you to it,' he said, placing the tray on the table. 'I'll see you later, Margot.'

'Yes, thanks.'

'If you could give me your contact details before you go, Mr Evans, in case we need to speak to you.'

'Why? What's happened?'

'It's routine.'

Whitney pulled out her notepad and handed it over to him with a pen. 'Please jot down your phone number on there, and then you may go.'

He looked at her, then took the notepad, did as he was asked and left the room.

Whitney picked up a mug of coffee and took a sip, waiting a few seconds before speaking to ensure Evans was out of earshot.

'Mrs Hargrove, we're not yet releasing to the public that

your husband's death wasn't from natural causes, so we'd ask you to keep it to yourself for now.'

'What about my daughter? She's coming round later. She was in Spain when we received the news about her father, and she came straight back.'

'Yes, of course you may explain to her,' Whitney confirmed.

'Was she particularly close to her father?' George asked.

'Fairly, but not overly. Jonathan wasn't really close to anyone, to be perfectly honest, because of his work.'

'Had he always been so dedicated?' Whitney asked. 'Does that mean that he didn't spend much time with you?'

Mrs Hargrove gave a hollow laugh. 'We lived separate lives, to be honest. But that was how it was. Occasionally, I'd accompany him if there was a function he was attending that was for partners also, and vice versa for my parish councils and committee. Sometimes I asked him to join me. But other than that, we pretty much kept to ourselves. When he was at work, I didn't see him, obviously. And when he was at home, he spent most of his time in his study.'

'Had he received any threats recently?'

'Not that I know of. Like I said, he didn't confide in me.'

'Okay. I'd like to ask you about Ted Evans?' Whitney said, sitting back in her chair, wanting to make it seem less like an interrogation and more like a chat. She thought it was the best approach, because there was definitely more to their friendship than met the eye. 'He seemed very familiar with the house and you.'

'He's a good friend,' she said, colouring slightly.

'And there's nothing more to the relationship?' Whitney probed.

'Not really,' she said.

'Can you be more explicit?'

'I know he likes me, and I like him, but we're both married. Or, I was married. But he's been very kind. He's a good friend.'

'I see. I'd like to ask a few more questions about Jonathan. Although he spent most of his time working, did he talk about his work at all? In particular, this latest theory of his, Death's Shadow?'

'He told me that he had what he referred to as a "groundbreaking theory" that was going to put him well and truly on the map.'

'I see. Did he explain it to you?'

'Not really. He said I wouldn't understand it.' She shook her head. 'Even though we were at Oxford together, he could be somewhat disparaging, simply because I wasn't as scientific as him.'

'You were at Oxford?'

'Yes.'

'Does he still keep in touch with any of his former fellow students?'

'Not that I know of.'

George leant forwards inquisitively. 'Where did he undertake his postgrad studies?'

Mrs Hargrove brightened a bit. 'He did a master's in Jungian and post-Jungian studies at Essex University, and also his PhD in depth psychology, with an emphasis on archetypes and collective unconscious.'

Whitney glanced uncertainly at George, who nodded thoughtfully, steepling her fingers, clearly appearing to understand the terminology.

'And his postdoctoral research?' George asked.

'He spent a year at the C.G. Jung Institute in Zurich doing further research into Jungian concepts.'

'In particular the "shadow" and how it manifests,' George stated.

'Yes. That's right.' Mrs Hargrove tilted her head. 'You're a psychologist?'

'Forensic psychology is my field,' George explained.

Whitney leant forward. 'Did he keep in contact with any of his colleagues?'

Mrs Hargrove shook her head. 'Not that I know of. If he did, he didn't mention it to me.'

'What about friends?' Whitney pressed further. 'Who can we talk to?'

Sighing, Mrs Hargrove crossed her arms protectively. 'He had no time for friends. He was a bit of a loner.'

Whitney and George exchanged a look. 'Okay, so no friends,' Whitney clarified. 'But no threats?'

'No.' Mrs Hargrove glanced away.

'We'd like to have a look around his study, if we may?' Whitney asked gently.

'Yes, of course.' Mrs Hargrove rose slowly and motioned for them to follow.

She led them down the hall towards the back of the house into a dim room lined with packed bookcases and centred around a large mahogany desk. Whitney quickly pulled some disposable gloves from her bag and handed a pair to George before beginning to look around.

'Is there anything in here that looks out of place?' Whitney asked Mrs Hargrove.

'No, not that I can think of. The last time he was in here would have been Saturday evening. No, Sunday morning, before he left. He said he wanted to do some last-minute preparations on his presentation.'

'We have the laptop that he had with him at the conference. Did he use any other computer at all?'

'No, he always worked on that.'

'Okay, thanks. If you could go back into the sitting room, we'll find you when we've finished,' Whitney said.

Mrs Hargrove left them, and they looked around. The room was very tidy. George was staring at the bookcases. 'I think he's got every text ever written on serial killers,' she said, peering at the spines. 'Including those he wrote himself. In fact, he has several copies of each of those.'

'You've read his work?'

'No,' George said.

Whitney looked through the drawers, but there was nothing out of the ordinary.

'What do you make of Mrs Hargrove? When we explained who we were, did you think her reaction was genuine?'

'No, it wasn't. Not at all. Her body language seemed forced. I think she believed she had to act distressed because her husband had died. In my opinion, it hasn't made much difference to her. Does that make her one of our suspects?'

'We can't rule her out,' Whitney said. 'I'd be surprised if it was her. I mean, we'll check CCTV, but she would have had to drive there in the morning, inject him, and then leave without being seen. Let's go back. There's nothing here to assist us.'

They headed back to the sitting room, where Mrs Hargrove was standing by the window, with one hand on the mantelpiece.

She turned as they entered. 'Was there anything in there to help?'

Whitney shook her head. 'No. I do have one further question, though. What were you doing yesterday between the hours of eleven in the morning and two-thirty in the afternoon?'

'I was here. My cleaner works on a Monday between eleven and two. I know some people like to go out when their cleaners are there but I prefer to be around in case she has any questions, or to see what's going on.'

Whitney jotted a note. 'Okay, and your cleaner can vouch for you?'

'Yes, of course.' Mrs Hargrove nodded firmly.

'Had she gone by the time you found out about your husband?' Whitney clarified.

'Yes.' Mrs Hargrove looked down, twisting a ring on her

finger, her voice quieting. 'I had a visit from a police officer in the afternoon to let me know what had happened, and then I was taken to identify Jonathan.'

Whitney stepped forwards sympathetically. 'We'll leave you now. Is there anyone that can be with you? It's obviously a bit of a shock now you know what's really happened.'

Mrs Hargrove gave a small shake of her head, not meeting their eyes. 'I'll be fine until Ted comes back, but thank you. My daughter will be here soon, too.'

'We'll be sending a family liaison officer to be with you,' Whitney explained gently. 'They will let you know what's going on with the investigation.'

Mrs Hargrove looked up, brow furrowing. 'I don't need one. I'll be fine.'

'It's a matter of routine,' Whitney said firmly but not unkindly. She handed Mrs Hargrove her card. 'If you do have any questions in the meantime…'

Mrs Hargrove took the card, glancing at it briefly. 'And Ted? May I tell him?'

'If you can vouch for him, then okay. We don't wish to alert the person who committed the offence that we're aware of what really happened…'

Understanding dawned on Mrs Hargrove's face and she gave a small nod. 'Okay, I understand.'

'You stay there – we'll see ourselves out,' Whitney said, as they turned to go.

SIX

Tuesday

When they arrived at the conference centre reception there was a different man behind the desk. Whitney held out her ID and asked to see the manager.

'I'll call her,' the receptionist said, pressing one of the keys on the phone in front of him.

After a couple of minutes, a woman wearing a navy trouser suit headed out from behind the desk and walked over to them. She wore a badge reading *Janalyn Prude – Manager*.

'Good morning,' Whitney said. 'We're here regarding the unfortunate death of one of your patrons, Jonathan Hargrove.'

Janalyn frowned. 'Is there an issue?'

'Is there somewhere quiet we can talk?' Whitney asked, not wanting to discuss the matter in full view of people walking through the area.

'Yes, of course. Come to my office.'

The woman led them behind reception and into a room with a desk in one corner and a sofa and two easy chairs in another. She nodded for Whitney and George to sit.

'How can I help you?'

'This isn't public knowledge and we'd like to keep it that way, but we're investigating the death of Professor Hargrove. It's now been classified as suspicious,' Whitney began, keeping her voice low, to emphasise the importance of her words.

'Oh, my goodness. I didn't expect you to say that.' Janalyn clenched both fists in her lap.

'Could you tell me a little more about how the body was found? Were you on duty yesterday when the alarm was raised?'

'Yes, I was. One of the conference organisers, Emily Davies, found him in his room and called down to reception asking for an ambulance. I went straight up there and saw him lying on the bed. He looked so… you know… sort of normal lying there. I'd wondered if it was a heart attack or something.'

'We'd like to speak to Ms Davies; please could you arrange for someone to fetch her. We'll question her in here, if that's okay with you,' Whitney asked.

'Of course. Leave it with me.'

Janalyn left them alone in her office and after a few minutes, the door opened, and a woman in her late twenties walked in. She was wearing a pair of black trousers and a striped shirt over the top. She had blonde hair pulled back from her face into a scrunchie.

'Hello, I'm Emily Davies. You wanted to see me? Is there something wrong?' Her teeth lightly grazed her lower lip.

'Hello, Emily. We just want to talk to you about Jonathan Hargrove. You're the person who found him yesterday?'

'Oh my God, it was awful. I can still picture it. It's the first time I've seen a dead body,' she said, the words tumbling out of her mouth.

'Have a seat. It can't have been easy for you,' Whitney said. She waited until the woman was seated. 'Because Professor Hargrove's death happened away from his home and was unexpected, we do have to investigate. It's standard procedure,' Whitney said.

'I understand.'

'First of all, please could you explain your role here at the conference?'

'I'm one of the organisers,' Emily said, brightening slightly. 'I help ensure everything runs smoothly. The conference speakers all seem to have their own requirements, in particular for PowerPoint presentations. Some of them can be quite demanding.' She paused for a couple of seconds as if replaying in her mind her reply. 'Not that I'm saying anything against them – I understand their work is precious to them and they want to make sure nothing goes wrong.'

'Are you able to attend the sessions?' George asked, assuming that would be a perk of the position.

'Yes, I am. That's one of the reasons why I wanted to be an organiser. I couldn't afford it otherwise.'

'What were your other reasons?' George asked, interested to discover what they were.

'Um... well, there's the networking. Meeting other criminologists. Like you.' Emily glanced down, a slight flush to her cheeks.

'You know of Dr Cavendish?' Whitney asked, glancing quickly at George, a glint in her eye.

'Of course. Who wouldn't.'

'What's your background?' Whitney asked.

'I'm a psychology PhD student.'

'Did you attend Professor Hargrove's session on Sunday?' George asked.

'Yes, I did. It was very interesting, but...' She glanced either side of Whitney and George as if about to divulge a secret. 'It did cause a few unexpected issues.'

'Really? What were they?' Whitney asked.

'Professor Hargrove had a Q and A session after the main

presentation of his paper. There was one attendee who was extremely rude, asked pointed questions, and tried to criticise the theory.'

'That's not unheard of during a research conference,' George said.

'It was more than what you'd usually expect to hear. Everyone was talking about it afterwards.'

'Who was this critic?' Whitney asked.

'Dr McDonnell.'

'Angus McDonnell?' George asked, frowning in recognition of the name.

'Yes, that's him.' Emily nodded.

George turned to Whitney. 'He works in the Lenchester University psychology department.'

'How did Professor Hargrove respond?' Whitney asked.

'He was very good. Every criticism Dr McDonnell came up with, Professor Hargrove had an answer. And he didn't lose his cool... at least not during the Q and A session.'

'What do you mean by that?' Whitney asked, exchanging a glance with George.

'I saw them first thing Monday morning, standing in the corridor having what looked like a very heated discussion.'

'Could you hear what it was about?' Whitney asked.

'No. I didn't stop to listen. I went into the restaurant for breakfast. I was late getting up and only had ten minutes before my shift started. I'm required to be around to deal with any problems.'

'I see. Why were you in Professor Hargrove's room when you found him?'

'He'd asked for some papers relating to other speakers at the conference to be brought to his room. I knocked on the door but there was no answer. I knocked again, and pushed the door open – it hadn't caught on the latch. I poked my head in, thinking I'd leave the papers on the table, and saw him there. At first, I wondered if he was asleep, so I called out to him, but he didn't answer. I went over because he didn't look right. He definitely wasn't asleep because there was no movement at all.' Emily's voice trembled as she recounted what had happened.

'What did you do then?' Whitney pushed.

'I picked up the phone and called down to reception.' Her hand mimicked the motion of making the call. 'The manager came up, took one look at the professor and told me he was dead.'

'And then?'

'I was sort of in shock, but went onto autopilot and returned to the conference and told the other organisers what had happened.'

'Did you see anyone hanging around near the room?' Whitney asked.

'No. I don't think so.'

'Okay, thank you for your help. You can go back to the conference,' Whitney said.

Emily left the room and Whitney turned to George. 'Tell me about McDonnell. How well do you know him?' Whitney leant back in her chair, crossing her arms, and focusing intently on George.

'I don't know him personally. He's applied to the research committee for ethical consideration of some research he's undertaking. I was saving reading through his application until closer to our next meeting, or at least until after the wedding.'

'What's his research on?'

'It's similar to Hargrove's. He's investigating serial killers from a psychological perspective.'

'Right, let's speak to him.'

They went out to the reception desk, where Janalyn Prude was assisting the receptionist. 'We'd like to talk to one of the conference delegates, Angus McDonnell,' Whitney said.

'I imagine he'll still be in the main opening session – they haven't broken out yet.'

'Please can you send someone in and ask for Dr McDonnell to come to reception without saying why.'

'I'll do it myself,' the manager said. They waited a few minutes, until finally she returned. 'Sorry, he's not here. I understand from his colleague that he's at work and won't be attending the conference until later today.'

'Okay, thanks,' Whitney said. She turned to George. 'We need to get to Lenchester University pronto.'

SEVEN

Tuesday

George drove through the gates leading to the university and parked in her designated spot.

'You're very lucky to work here. It's beautiful,' Whitney remarked, staring at the ancient oak trees whose gnarled branches reached out as if they were touching the sky.

'Yes, I agree,' George said, her voice soft. 'I wish I had more time to enjoy the grounds because they're delightful. We have some beautiful beech trees lining the perimeter, and there's a lovely pond which they've been cultivating over the last few years.'

'I wish I was into gardening like you are,' Whitney said wistfully. 'I can barely manage to mow the lawn. But then again, there isn't time for everything. The main thing is we've got a play area for Ava and somewhere for us to sit outside if we ever get some decent weather. Although with climate change, we are getting sunnier days.'

'I find gardening extremely therapeutic. Except it's hard to keep on top of the large garden we now have.'

'Doesn't Ross help?'

Surely they shared it? Whitney would be surprised if they didn't.

'Of course. I leave him to mow the lawn and I deal with the flower beds and the pruning because he can get a bit heavy-handed when it comes to that.'

'You surprise me. With him being a sculptor, I'd have thought he'd be very gentle. In fact, I thought you might've turned all your hedges into objects like rabbits, balls, or different animals. You know... What do they call that sort of thing?'

'I believe you're referring to topiary.'

'Yes, that's it,' Whitney said, with a nod.

'As popular as that might be, I can assure you my hedges will be perfectly straight and symmetrical. I also like to leave parts of the garden wild – it's enjoyable to see a haphazard mass of colour.'

Whitney couldn't help noticing how relaxed George's facial expression became when discussing her garden, in contrast to how tense it seemed to be most of the time at present. And people said that weddings are meant to be the best day of your life. Well, she'd certainly reserve judgement on that, if her friend was anything to go by.

'I'll take your word for it,' Whitney said, removing her seat belt and opening the car door. She stepped out into the fresh air, enjoying the warmth of the sun on her face. 'Let's find Angus McDonnell. Do you know where his office is?'

'No, but we'll ask the college administrator in his department.'

They headed through the main entrance of one of the older brick buildings and down a long corridor until reaching the sign indicating they'd reached the Department of Psychology.

'Leave me to speak. I don't want to alarm anyone that the police are here,' George said.

'Okay.'

They walked into the administrator's office and Whitney stayed by the door.

'I'm looking for Angus McDonnell,' George said as the administrator glanced up at her. 'Can you tell me his room number? It will save me from having to trek up and down the corridors.'

'You'll find him in B-21, Dr Cavendish. Turn left when you leave my office. Go to the end of the corridor. Turn right, and his room will be on the left.'

'Lovely, thank you very much.' George smiled.

As they left the office, Whitney slowed down, staring up at one of the large portraits that lined the halls of the older buildings.

'Bloody hell,' Whitney said, pointing up. 'I'd hate to be taught by him. He looks very scary.'

'A portrait is no indication of a lecturer's effectiveness, Whitney. Surely you realise that.'

Whitney shrugged. George was right. It was probably that she felt intimidated every time she entered the university. Which was ridiculous. She'd been on track for university entrance before falling pregnant with Tiffany. Studying for a degree was on her bucket list, but that would have to wait until retirement.

They followed the directions given by the administrator and soon arrived at McDonnell's office. The door was slightly ajar and Whitney could see movement in the gap.

'He's there,' she said.

George tapped twice on the frosted glass.

'Come in.'

Inside, a man in his fifties with a shaved head peered over the top of his laptop at them. He was wearing brown corduroy trousers and a navy sweater.

'Dr Cavendish, how can I help you?' he asked with a gap-toothed ingratiating smile.

Clearly, he was creeping around George because of his work being in front of the research committee.

Whitney took an instant dislike to him.

They strode over to where he was sitting.

'Good morning, Angus. This is Detective Chief Inspector Walker from Lenchester CID. We'd like to have a word with you about the death of Jonathan Hargrove.'

'Yes, that was awful, wasn't it? I heard about it yesterday. Why are the police involved?' he asked with a frown.

'Standard procedure,' Whitney said, batting off his question with a flick of her hand. 'Why aren't you at the conference now?'

'Take a seat,' he said, gesturing to the two chairs next to his desk. They sat down and waited for him to answer. 'I had a meeting this morning with a colleague and I have some marking to complete, but I'm intending to attend some of the afternoon sessions, if I can.'

'We'd like to ask you about the presentation of Hargrove's paper on Sunday. You were there, I believe?' Whitney said.

He glanced away, not making eye contact. 'Yes, that's correct.'

'I understand from witnesses that you were antagonistic towards him during the Q and A.'

'You may call it that. I would call it academic debate,' McDonnell said, shifting about in his chair and peering over their heads.

Clear avoidance. What was he hiding?

'Whatever it's called, I think you'll agree that it was *difficult*. We were also informed that there was a heated exchange between the two of you on Monday morning, prior to breakfast,' Whitney continued.

'Gosh, you have had your spies out, haven't you?' He tutted. 'But they don't know what they're talking about. Yes, I asked Jonathan a few pointed questions on Sunday, and rightly so. As for Monday morning, let's say we resumed our conversation. That's all there is to it. Look, I'd known the man for years and we had that sort of relationship.'

'How long?' Whitney asked, jumping on the admission.

'We were at Oxford together.'

'Were you friends?' she asked.

If they were, he hardly seemed bothered by the man's recent demise.

'Not really. If anything, you could call us rivals. In an academic sense, and there's nothing wrong with that. Isn't that right, Dr Cavendish?' he said, turning his attention to George.

'Academic rivalry isn't unusual,' George acknowledged.

McDonnell nodded. 'See? Look, I'm sorry that Jonathan died, but I don't see why you're questioning me about it.'

'You thought his theory was controversial, didn't you?' George said, asking her first question.

'Yes, I did.'

'Why was that?'

'Because it's more speculative than scientific, and, if adopted, could prove to be ethically problematic. I don't believe he thought through the theory's implications carefully enough. I'm not saying that there aren't worthwhile components to his theory, because there absolutely are, and it could revolutionise our understanding of serial killers. But I also believe that he was too narrow-minded in his view, at the expense of considering other options and some of the difficulties.'

'I see,' Whitney said, sort of understanding what he was saying. George could enlighten her, anyway. 'What were you doing between eleven in the morning and two-thirty yesterday afternoon?'

'I was at the conference.' He glanced upwards. 'Actually, no, I wasn't. I came back here to try to catch up on some marking. I saw the opening paper, "Social Control and Criminal Justice", but didn't go to any of the breakout sessions.'

'Did you stay overnight on Sunday at the conference after Professor Hargrove's presentation?' George asked.

'No, I went home. But arrived early to have a breakfast meeting.'

'With whom and for what?' George asked.

'Dr Inman. We were discussing the possibility of undertaking some research together. It's very early days and we haven't yet firmed up our topic.'

'And you happened to bump into Jonathan Hargrove on the way in?' Whitney asked.

'Yes, that's correct.' He gave a sharp nod.

'Who started the conversation?' Whitney asked, cocking her head to one side.

'He did. He wanted to go over our discussion on Sunday night.'

'Why would he do that if it was simply healthy academic debate?' Whitney challenged.

'Because that's the sort of person he was. He never could take criticism.'

'Where exactly were you between eleven and two-thirty?' Whitney asked, steering the conversation back.

'Here, in my office.' He panned his hand from side to side.

'Can anyone vouch for you?' Whitney asked. She leant forwards in her chair and stared directly at Dr McDonnell.

He couldn't maintain eye contact and he looked away. 'No, because I was on my own.'

'Didn't you see anyone in the corridors?' George asked.

'Term hasn't started and there aren't any students hanging around.'

'Staff?' George asked, arching an eyebrow.

He shrugged. 'I don't remember.'

'How come you've got marking when there are no students?' Whitney asked.

'I run distance-learning courses, and those assignments are

submitted at different times from the full-time students. I was working on some of those.'

'And the timestamps on the documents on your laptop will corroborate—?'

'Well, possibly not,' McDonnell interrupted. 'Because I might've just been reading them at that time, and not making any comments.'

Whitney glanced at George, who clearly wasn't buying it either.

'That all seems very vague,' she said.

'It's the truth.'

'Did you see anything suspicious at the conference that, with hindsight, indicated Jonathan Hargrove could be in danger?'

'Why are you saying *danger*? Didn't he die of natural causes?'

'We're investigating all possibilities,' Whitney said, not wanting to tell the man the truth about Hargrove's demise. She didn't reckon he'd keep it a secret for long.

'So, you're asking questions of everybody, is that right?'

'People who have been brought to our notice,' Whitney replied. 'We were informed about the two of you falling out and wished to pursue it further.'

'It's not a question of us falling out, as you put it. It was simply academic rigour, as Dr Cavendish will verify.' He glanced at George but her expression remained impassive. 'I've known the man for years and, obviously, I'm sorry that he's dead. But our relationship has nothing to do with it. My guess is that he died because of his poor lifestyle. Overeating and too much drinking.'

'Are you saying that his behaviour was excessive?' George asked.

'I don't know. He didn't look like an overweight drunk, that's for sure. But he certainly enjoyed his life, so I believe.'

Whitney glanced at George, giving a nod towards the door. They were done here.

'We may wish to speak to you again, and I'd rather you kept this discussion to yourself, please,' Whitney said. 'We don't wish to alarm people when there's most likely no need.'

'No, of course not. I hope you get to the bottom of his death, but I'm sure there's nothing untoward to it.'

They left his room and headed back the way they'd come.

'Well?' Whitney asked George when they were far enough away for the man not to overhear.

'He dismissed his confrontation with Jonathan Hargrove as being nothing out of the ordinary, but it was obvious in his eyes the disdain he had for the man. They might have known each other for years, but they certainly weren't friends. That doesn't mean that he murdered him.'

'Are such heated arguments between academics common?' Whitney asked, with a frown.

'Oh yes,' George said thoughtfully. 'Academics can be quite vicious with each other when they want to be. If they think that a theory or paper being presented has faults, they will point them out without hesitation. Education is a competitive world and many researchers are very sensitive to criticism.'

'Are you?' Whitney asked.

'What do you think?' George asked, shaking her head.

'Sorry, stupid question. Do you think the disagreement about this Death's Shadow theory could have something to do with Hargrove's death?' Whitney asked.

'The disagreements took place in the open for people to see. If McDonnell was intent on murdering Hargrove, surely he'd be careful enough to not let anyone consider him a potential suspect?'

'In theory, yes. But we know from the past that doesn't always translate. We need to get back to the station and start looking into him. Is that okay with you, or do you want to go to the conference?'

'I'll come with you. I don't intend to return to the conference until Wednesday for the panel. There's nothing on today that piques my interest.'

'Okay,' Whitney said. 'I'll text Ellie and ask her to get started on researching Angus McDonnell. Hopefully, by the time we get back there, we might have more to work on.'

EIGHT

Tuesday

'Okay, everyone,' Whitney began, commanding everyone's attention. 'Let's have an update on where we are. George and I have interviewed Dr Angus McDonnell, a lecturer at Lenchester University, who was at the conference and was twice seen in confrontation with the victim. The first time was during a Q and A session following Hargrove's presentation on Sunday, and the second time, the following morning outside the restaurant during breakfast. He was spotted by one of the conference organisers.'

Whitney approached the whiteboard, removing the top from the marker. With a deliberate motion, she wrote McDonnell's name, then drew an arrow pointing from it to the victim's name.

She turned back to the team. 'Ellie, you were tasked with looking into McDonnell. Have you discovered anything useful?'

Ellie leant slightly forwards in her chair, a familiar crease forming on her forehead, which signalled deep concentration.

'Not really. He went to Oxford, and after graduating completed a PhD at Bristol where he lectured in criminology until moving to Lenchester University four years ago, to the psychology department. My focus so far has been on his work history. Aside from that, Professor Hargrove had a research assistant called Dr Toby Merchant. I've checked, and he's at the conference.'

'Excellent. Thanks. We'll get in touch with Merchant. For now, keep on digging into McDonnell. Look into his personal life and his social media presence. Anybody else got anything to share?'

From the corner of the room, Brian cleared his throat, anticipation evident in his posture. 'Actually, yes, guv,' he said, holding up a mobile. 'I went through Hargrove's phone and found several heated message exchanges between him and a Dr Valerie Jenkins.'

The room seemed to buzz with newfound energy, and Whitney felt a pulse of anticipation. 'What about?'

Brian swiped the screen, finding the exact messages. 'Three weeks ago, Jenkins messaged Hargrove saying that his work lacked empirical evidence, was ethically problematic, that there was a potential for stereotyping, and it didn't fit with other theories.'

Whitney felt a jolt, sensing the tension behind the words. She looked over at George, who was standing close by, seeking her insight. 'Well, thoughts?'

George's brow furrowed. 'Interesting that she chose the phrase "ethically problematic", which were McDonnell's exact words.'

'Coincidence?' Whitney asked, half tongue-in-cheek, knowing her colleague's view on that.

'It's not unusual for those words to be used in academic circles, however...' George trailed off, in thought.

'Okay, but could Jenkins and McDonnell have discussed

the theory in the past and he repeated what she'd said?' Whitney suggested.

'It's certainly possible and worth investigating. Dr Jenkins is attending the conference – she's on tomorrow's panel with me.'

'That's good to know. Brian, how did Hargrove respond?' Whitney asked, returning her attention to the messages.

'He said that her criticisms were unfounded and the only reason she was making them was because she was jealous of the attention his work was getting.'

'And her response?'

Brian hesitated a fraction, intensifying the suspense. 'She said they'd see about that and that she would make sure everyone knew that his work on Death's Shadow was not what he professed it to be.'

Whitney felt the gravity of the situation settling on her. 'We need to question Dr Valerie Jenkins – that message makes her a potential suspect.'

'I suggest we wait until tomorrow's panel. Keep it low-key. If she thinks that we're on to her, then she might disappear,' George said.

'I agree,' Whitney said, leaning against one of the empty desks. The soft hum of the overhead lights filled her ears. 'I wonder how all this fits with McDonnell? Could they have been working together to discredit Hargrove... or kill him even?'

'Not necessarily,' George replied, rubbing the back of her neck. 'There are several people unhappy with Hargrove's theory, not just McDonnell and Jenkins.'

'Guv,' Ellie suddenly called out, her voice slicing through the thick atmosphere, drawing all eyes towards her. She looked up from her computer screen. 'Something's popped up in my search but I don't know if it's relevant or not. McDonnell, whilst at Oxford University, won the Hamilton Medal.'

'Did he, indeed?' George exclaimed, her eyebrows arching

in genuine surprise. 'The Hamilton Medal is an extremely prestigious award and an excellent achievement. I had no idea that McDonnell was a recipient. He certainly doesn't put it on any of his credentials when applying for research grants, which is most surprising.'

'Would most people do that?' Whitney asked, an image of McDonnell flashing across her mind. He hadn't come across as being so self-effacing that he wouldn't show off his awards.

'Oh yes, of course. It shows a high level of academic attainment.'

'So why would he leave it off his CV?' Whitney asked, hoping George might have some insight.

'I can't say, but it's something we should address,' George replied.

'Agreed. Good work, Ellie. Now, what about the CCTV, Frank?' Whitney asked.

'Doug and I checked the conference centre footage. We've looked at the lifts, around reception, at various people coming and going from the actual conference rooms. Nothing in particular stands out as concerning,' Frank said, his fingers intertwined.

A pang of frustration coursed through Whitney, her grip on the marker pen tightening. Why couldn't anything be straightforward?

'Did you look through footage in the accommodation section?' George asked.

Frank shook his head slowly. 'No we didn't. Come to think of it, they didn't send any footage from there, so either the cameras aren't recording, or they didn't realise you wanted to see that, too.'

Whitney gave a frustrated sigh. 'Okay, we'll need to speak to them about that. Next steps. Tomorrow we'll question the research assistant and also Valerie Jenkins, but we'll wait until after the panel to speak to her as you suggested.' She glanced at George. 'What time's the panel?'

'Two in the afternoon.'

'Okay, tomorrow morning we'll also speak to Merchant and arrange for CCTV footage from the accommodation areas to be sent. I'm off to speak to Superintendent Clyde to let her know what's going on. I emailed her earlier about it and she's asked me for an update in person. I'll suggest that there's no need for a press conference yet. It will work in our favour to keep this low-key.'

Whitney left the incident room and headed to her boss's office. She knocked gently on the door.

'Come in,' the superintendent called.

Whitney took a moment to compose herself, straightening her posture and clearing her throat before walking in. 'I'm here for the update regarding the suspicious death of Professor Hargrove, ma'am.'

Clyde leant forwards, giving her full attention. 'Thanks, Whitney. What's the situation?'

'There are a couple of possible suspects, but nothing concrete. I don't believe we need a press conference because the incident seems self-contained in the conference centre and I believe it's best to keep low-key for now. I made the decision to allow the conference to continue as planned because, if the murderer is there, as far as they're concerned, they've got away with it. Although we'll be interviewing delegates and explaining that it's standard procedure when someone dies unexpectedly away from their home.'

The superintendent nodded slowly, tapping a single finger on her desk. 'Good, you appear to have it all under control. Let me know if you need me to do anything, and hopefully, this will be solved soon.'

'Thanks, ma'am,' Whitney replied, relieved that the super agreed with her plan of action.

She turned and left the office, the weight of the case pressing down on her once more.

As she headed back to the incident room, her phone buzzed in her pocket. Pulling it out, she saw Tiffany's name flash on the screen. Her heart softened, a respite from the chaos.

'Hello, Mum,' came her daughter's voice, soft with a hint of excitement. 'What time are you coming home this evening? I'd like to go out for a drink with some friends and I wondered if you could look after Ava?'

Whitney sighed internally. The never-ending balancing act of being a detective and a mother. 'Yes, I can do that. I'm working on a case, but not doing anything further now until tomorrow. I need to be in work early, so I don't want you out too late.'

'Noted. It's just a drink with some old uni friends,' Tiffany said, a hint of laughter in her voice. 'I wanted to catch up with them, now I know I'll be returning.'

Whitney smiled. 'That's fine. So, what have you been up to today?'

'I took Ava to kindergarten, and then spent the next three hours in the library, reading. I'm trying to get back up to speed with everything. I'm really nervous about going back.'

Whitney's heart ached, sensing her daughter's apprehension. 'You'll be fine. You did well before. There's no reason for you not to do so again.'

'I hope so. But what if I've forgotten everything?'

'It will soon come back to you when you start going to classes and doing your assignments. Don't worry about it,' Whitney reassured her, hoping to instil some confidence. 'I'd better go. I'll be home soon.'

Whitney returned to the incident room, ready to wrap up the day and prepare for the next.

'Okay, everyone, let's make it an early night because tomorrow we're going to be busy.' Whitney's voice was full of hope that the next day they would discover information to help them solve the case.

George, who was leaning against a desk, chatting with Ellie, looked up. Their eyes met, a silent agreement of the weight of the task ahead. 'I'll be here first thing,' her friend acknowledged with a nod.

NINE

Tuesday

George closed the front door behind her and gave a loud sigh.

What a day.

Compartmentalising was her special skill, but this week was challenging even her. She glanced up as Ross came out of the kitchen holding a glass of red wine.

She hung up her coat on one of the hooks in the porch and took it from him.

'Thanks,' she said, taking a long sip and welcoming its smoothness as it slipped down her throat. 'Never have I need this more.'

'What's wrong?' he asked, concerning flickering in his eyes.

'Believe it or not, we now have a suspicious death to investigate. I thought I had everything relating to my work organised until after the wedding. I didn't factor in a murder. It's most frustrating.'

'Surely Whitney can work the case without you, especially as she knows that we've got so much to sort out?'

'That's not possible. The murder occurred at the conference I'm currently attending – an area that I'm very familiar with.'

'An academic's been murdered?' Ross said, his eyes wide. 'Can you tell me anything about it?'

'Of course not.' She frowned as they headed into the kitchen.

Ross chuckled. 'I realised as soon as I asked what your reply would be.'

She had to admit, living with Ross had been the best thing she'd ever done. He could read her like no one else had ever done. He knew exactly how she was feeling and understood her need to be left alone when she was busy. He never complained when she was absorbed in something, be it working with Whitney or her research projects.

Although, it cut both ways. When he was engrossed in one of his sculptures, and had a lot of work on, she knew not to disturb him. As Whitney would say, it was a match made in heaven. Although, it was unlikely that her parents would agree. They'd met Ross on several occasions, and although initially they weren't very welcoming towards him, the last few times they'd seen them, they'd been more convivial. It probably helped that her father, who had Parkinson's and had been forced to give up his lucrative private practice as a world-renowned heart surgeon, had become a little more understanding and tolerant.

Not that it bothered her. She'd never been particularly close to her parents, nor her brother, who was a chip off her father's block and was establishing himself as a well-respected surgeon in his own right.

It was very different with Ross and his family, who, to be honest, she found a tad overwhelming, with their constant desire to hug at every opportunity. But they'd been nothing but welcoming to her and she endured their overly touchiness without, she hoped, letting on how awkward it made her feel.

She'd mentioned what they're like to Whitney, and her friend had said it was thanks to them being friends that George was now able to navigate being with the *common people*. George denied it, of course. Whitney had simply laughed.

'What time's dinner?' she asked.

'Now. I thought you'd like to eat early so we can continue sorting out a last-minute arrangement for the wedding that need addressing.'

'What last-minute arrangement? We've done the seating plan. Has something occurred that I'm not aware of?' George grimaced.

'I had a phone call from my mother and it turns out that her sister Vi can attend after all.'

'Your sister Vi?' George asked, trying to recollect the woman and failing.

'No, my *aunt* Vi,' Ross said.

'Okay, that makes more sense. I get confused with your family members, there are so many of them.' And that was an understatement.

'True. And none of them can be excluded, as you know, because it would cause a massive rift in the family that could go on for years.'

George had to take his word for that because her family was so small and kept to themselves. She had some cousins she'd only ever met once or twice in her entire life... not that she wanted to see them more.

'You can make the decision where to place your aunt as I have no idea of where would be appropriate,' she said, shrugging.

'I was considering putting her on the table with Whitney.'

'Why would we do that?' George asked, not understanding his rationale. It made no sense at all.

'Because I think they'll get on well together and, most importantly, there's an odd number on her table.'

'Your family are very close, so I think we should keep them together.'

'That's easier said than done. We could always move your pathologist and her husband, and instead put Vi there with another of my aunts?' He ran his fingers through his hair. 'Who knew seating plans could be so difficult? Let's wait until after dinner to discuss it. I don't think it's a decision I can make alone. It's not easy.'

'Okay,' George said with a sigh. 'As long as we don't take too long, as I've other things to deal with.'

'No problem. Oh... and before I forget, Mum wants us to go out with them on the Friday evening, the day before the wedding. She'd like to plan a dinner for everyone. With all my family staying at the same hotel in Lenchester, she thought we could hold it there. What do you think? She wants to invite your family to join us so they have a chance to meet before the actual day.'

George swallowed hard. Even she realised it could be a difficult situation. But she didn't want to hurt the feelings of Ross's mother.

'I'm not sure that's a good idea, considering how outnumbered my family would be. It's only my parents, my brother and his wife.'

'I still don't understand why you didn't want to invite your extended family.'

George drew in a breath, measuring her words. She didn't want to upset Ross. 'This was meant to be a very small, intimate wedding. I accept that you have a large family, none of whom you wish to omit. But you know me better than anyone, and I have no desire to be surrounded by people I seldom see, and who are most likely going to judge others around them.'

'By others... you mean my family?' Ross said.

'You've met my parents – set in their ways and the epitome of snobbery. The rest of the family is identical. I'm not excusing their behaviour because there's no reason for them to be like that. Just explaining my decision.'

Ross gave a dry smile. 'It's not exactly a picnic in the park when we're with your family and I'm glad we don't see them often. No offence meant.'

'No offence taken,' George said with a smile. 'Come on, let's eat because I really do have work to do after we've finished with the seating plan.'

'Students haven't even started classes yet.' Ross frowned. 'What are you working on?'

'I need to prep for the upcoming term. Oh, and I've been asked to be the keynote speaker at a European conference in March next year.'

'That's months away.'

'Yes, but I must decide on a topic soon. It's for their marketing push.'

'Where's the conference?'

'Salzburg.'

'Well, then, let's make a holiday of it. We could call it a belated honeymoon.'

He stared at her with an expression she couldn't quite read. They'd talked about a honeymoon before, but between his commissions and her new academic year, they'd put their travel plans on hold. Still, Salzburg could be perfect for that long-awaited celebration.

'Excellent, that's what we'll do then,' she said, placing her glass of wine on the kitchen table.

Her phone rang, and she glanced at the screen.

'Oh, no,' she groaned.

'Who is it?'

'My brother. Shall I ignore it and return the call after dinner?'

'No, answer it now. Because then dinner being served will give you an excuse to end it.'

'Excellent idea,' she said, nodding. 'Hello, James.'

'Georgina, how are you and your partner?'

Her insides clenched. She hated anyone using her full name.

'I'm fine. So is Ross,' she emphasised. 'What can I help you with? We're about to eat.'

'At this time? It's rather early for an evening meal, isn't it?' She could imagine the way his top lip was turned up in disdain.

'We're busy, James. Now, I take it you phoned for a specific reason?'

'Yes, I have. I wish to discuss logistics concerning Mother and Father at the wedding.'

Why was it his concern?

'Explain what you mean,' she replied, keeping her voice steady.

'I'm not sure that Father's up to sitting on a top table. I suggest you seat him with Deanna and me. We'll be able to keep an eye on him and help Mother. His condition is worsening. He's dragging his right foot badly, and, despite medication, his movements are much slower and deliberate.'

'You're asking me to remove him from the top table? That would appear odd and I'm sure he wouldn't wish to draw attention to himself in that way.'

'I can help him if he is situated next to me. Maybe Deanna and I should be on the top table, too?'

'That's not possible. I will assist Father should it be necessary.'

James sighed loudly. 'Georgina, you're not fully medically trained and might not realise if there's an issue.'

She glanced over at Ross, who was staring at her, appearing concerned. She shook her head to let him know that it was under control. 'James, contrary to what you believe, I am well qualified in my profession and perfectly capable of ensuring that Father is okay whilst seated at the top table during the meal. Afterwards, if he wishes to sit with you and your wife, I'm sure we can arrange something.'

There was silence for a few seconds.

'How many people will be attending?' her brother finally said.

'Close to one hundred. It's small.'

Although not as small as she'd like, it was when compared with her brother's wedding, where there had been several hundred guests.

'Why do you need a top table with so few people attending? For such a small affair, I don't know why you're making it formal.'

Actually, maybe he's right, George admitted to herself. 'I'll give it some thought. How are you and Deanna?'

'We're fine, thank you. I'm extremely busy at work, and taking the time out to come to Lenchester has caused a few issues in terms of rearranging appointments.'

'The wedding is on a Saturday.'

'We're coming up the day before with Mother and Father.'

'At your level, I'm sure there's someone who can deputise.'

'My reputation is paramount. In the same way as it was for Father when he was working. He didn't like to entrust his private patients in the hands of anyone else.'

'James, I refuse to believe that your entire practice will fold because of you not being there for one day. I must go because my dinner's ready. I'll see you a week on Friday. There will be a dinner in the evening with Ross's family, which I expect you, Deanna and Mother and Father to attend.'

'I'm not prepared to commit at this stage. We'll discuss closer to the time.'

'It's not up for discussion. The meal will be booked and you're to attend,' George said, not prepared to let her brother get away with bamboozling her a moment longer. She was the elder of the two and he should respect that.

'Okay, if you insist,' James said, his voice resigned. 'We'll attend. The main thing is that you understand about Father.'

She ended the call and turned to Ross. 'My brother's concerned about my father's health and doesn't think he should be on a top table. I wasn't prepared to admit it to him but he might have a point. Do you think we should have round tables for everyone and then Mother and Father can be with James and his wife?'

Ross walked over to her and rested his hands on her shoulders.

'George, think about it. If we changed everything now, where would we sit? My parents would want to be with us, and having a top table is traditional. Don't let your brother cause you to second guess what we're doing.'

He was right.

'Yes. It's our wedding and we'll do it our way.'

TEN

Wednesday

'We'll go to the reception first because I want them to send over the CCTV footage from the accommodation side, immediately. I'll forward it to Frank and they can go through it whilst we're here,' Whitney said as George drove them to the conference centre the next morning.

'Yes... okay,' George muttered.

She glanced at her friend, who had a distant look in her eyes.

'Are you listening to me?' she asked, her concern growing as she turned to face her friend more directly. It was unlike George to be so detached, especially when discussing work.

George's eyes flicked to Whitney and then back to the road. 'Yes. You mentioned the CCTV.' Her voice was flat, her mind clearly elsewhere.

Whitney leant back in her seat, studying George's profile. 'Okay. But I can tell there's something on your mind. What is it? The wedding?' she probed, her voice softening, filled with concern.

George let out a heavy sigh, her shoulders slumping slightly. 'Yes. It's getting way out of hand,' she admitted, the stress evident.

'Tell me what's happened. It will help if you talk about it.' She noted the tension in George's face, the lines around her eyes, and her lips pressed into a thin line.

'Ross's mother wants a big family-get-together dinner the evening before. My brother is demanding that we don't have a top table so that he can take care of my father. Ross's aunt now wishes to attend after we have all the seating organised, and—'

'George, stop. What you're telling me is perfectly normal wedding planning issues. It's fine and will all be sorted out. Trust me,' she interjected, her voice firm, yet reassuring.

'How do you know this? You haven't been married,' George said, frowning in her direction.

'Ouch... Rub it in, why don't you?' Whitney joked, trying to lighten the mood.

'I'm sorry. That wasn't what I meant. I—'

'I was kidding. You're right, I haven't been married, but I've known plenty of people who have. Take a few deep breaths and don't let it bother you. Come on, you're great at compartmentalising. And this is a time when you should do that. Forget about everyone else. You do exactly as you want. It's your wedding and don't let anyone interfere. And if they do – like your brother – tell him where to get off.' Whitney thumped the dash. 'If you'd rather not do it, then you can delegate the responsibility to me, because I'll have no qualms in standing up for your rights.'

George turned, with a smile on her face. 'You're right, of course. We're here to work and I'm not going to let it get in the way.'

'Good. As I said, we'll head for the reception first, and then find Hargrove's research assistant.'

When they arrived at the conference centre, George parked

on the gravelled area at the front and they headed inside. On the way, George nodded at two people sitting in reception talking.

'Conference attendees,' she explained when Whitney looked over to see who they were.

When they reached the reception desk, the same man they'd seen yesterday was there.

'Good morning, DCI Walker, Dr Cavendish.'

'Hello, Wayne,' Whitney said, noticing his name badge. She didn't remember seeing it before but could have been wrong. 'I'm glad you're on duty; it saves me time.' She smiled. 'The CCTV footage you forwarded was only of the conference area. We'd like to see everything from the accommodation side, too, please.'

Wayne frowned. 'I'll have to check with Ms Prude, the manager.'

'Why?' Whitney demanded. 'We've already been sent some footage.'

'Because it's where people sleep. The manager is in the back office, so I won't be long.'

He turned, left the desk and headed out the back. After a minute, he returned.

'Well?' Whitney said.

'You can have it. Shall I send to the same email address as before?'

'Yes, please. Do it now. I want footage from first thing Sunday morning until Monday evening.'

'Consider it done,' the man said, his fingers on the keyboard.

'We'd like to speak to a Dr Toby Merchant who's attending the conference. Do you know where we can find him?'

'One of the conference organisers is over there,' Wayne said, nodding towards Emily Davies, who was standing close to the lift. 'She'll be able to help.'

'Thanks. I'd like a room to use for questioning. It doesn't

need to be big, but quiet and away from here. We won't need it for long.'

'The breakout rooms won't be used until eleven. You can have room one. It's to the right of the main room. The number's on the door.'

The phone rang, diverting his attention, and they hurried over to Emily Davies.

'Good morning,' Whitney said. 'We'd like to speak to Toby Merchant; do you know him?'

'Yes. He walked into the main conference room a few minutes ago. If you wait here, I'll fetch him.'

'Thanks. Tell him he has a visitor, but you don't know who. It will save time and won't alert other attendees, if they overhear.'

'Will do,' Emily said, hurrying away.

Whitney's phone pinged and she glanced at the screen. 'The footage has arrived. I'll forward it to Frank so they can work on it. They might have something for us by the time we get back there.'

After several minutes, Emily Davies reappeared accompanied by a man who looked to be in his late twenties. He wasn't very tall – only around five foot six – and he had dark hair pulled back off his face in a man bun. He was wearing light coloured jeans and a grey hoodie.

'Toby Merchant?' Whitney asked as the man got close.

'Yes, I'm *Dr* Merchant,' he replied, emphasising his title, and looking at Whitney and then George.

She swallowed back a facetious retort. If he was trying to impress, it wasn't working. George never tried to lord it over everyone with her academic title.

'I'm Detective Chief Inspector Walker and this is Dr Cavendish.'

'Ah... I thought I recognised you,' he said, looking at George, respect in his eyes. 'I understand that you're taking the place of Professor Hargrove on this afternoon's panel.'

'Yes, that's correct,' George said with a sharp nod.

'We're here to talk to you about Professor Hargrove. I've arranged the use of a breakout room where we can discuss matters in private,' Whitney said, turning away and beginning to head in the direction of the room to stop him from asking further questions until they were alone.

The breakout room had six rows of chairs, five seats in each, and at the head of the room was a table. Whitney pulled out three chairs so they could sit in a circle.

'Is there a problem?' Merchant asked once they were seated, looking decidedly uncomfortable at being there.

'It's standard procedure to talk to people who knew the deceased when their death was unexpected and occurred away from their home. I understand you were his research assistant,' Whitney replied, keeping her voice steady.

'Yes, that's correct,' Merchant said, puffing his chest out slightly.

Clearly, he believed it to be a great honour. George would confirm that for her later.

'What can you tell us about him? Had he been acting strange at all recently? Had he been concerned or stressed?' Whitney pulled out a notebook and pen from her pocket, and sat there, pen poised.

'I wouldn't say strange,' Merchant said, after a few moments' thought. 'He was always a difficult person to work with because he was so preoccupied with his work, and in particular more recently, after he'd published the paper on his Death's Shadow theory.'

'We understand this paper had many critics,' Whitney said.

'It had, but Jonathan believed in his theory. He knew that some people weren't going to like it, but that didn't bother him.

If anything, it made him more determined to prove his critics wrong.'

'So you wouldn't classify him as being stressed and in poor health?' Whitney checked.

'Absolutely not.'

'How do you feel about his theory, as his research assistant?' George asked.

Merchant looked directly at George. 'I understand the criticisms that were levelled at him, and maybe there were areas that needed further investigation, but I believe they could be overcome, and the theory will stand up, given the passage of time.'

'In respect of your role as his RA, how much input did you have in his research?' George continued.

'I did much of the data gathering and inputting the results into a reliable format.'

'Did you conduct any of the interviews for the professor?' George asked.

'Yes, I was part of that process. We undertook both qualitative and quantitative research for obvious reasons.'

Whitney glanced at George. She wasn't sure what the reasoning behind that was, having not undertaken any academic research. She was aware of the difference between research techniques from when she'd been studying for her sociology A level at school... until she dropped out after becoming pregnant.

George nodded and turned to her. 'Using both would give a much richer and more comprehensive picture, because it's a mix of data that can be used to generalise to larger populations, and rich, more in-depth accounts from individuals,' she said as if having read Whitney's mind.

'Thanks. Now Professor Hargrove's no longer with us, where does that leave you?' Whitney asked.

'I'll be continuing with the research because it's going to

make an important contribution to the field.' Merchant's voice was firm and determined.

Whitney frowned. 'Does that mean it will then be your theory and you'll take credit for it?' She might not be an academic, but that didn't seem right to her.

The man coloured slightly. 'It's not quite like that.'

Really?

'What is it like, then?'

'Professor Hargrove will be given posthumous credit for his input.'

'But you'll reap the benefits?' Whitney glanced at George, whose lips were turned up in a slight smile. Ah ha... she'd got it right.

'Possibly,' Merchant said, waving his hand dismissively.

'I want you to think carefully,' Whitney said, deciding to move the interview on. 'Was Professor Hargrove acting at all strange, or stranger than usual, over the last week or so?'

'He had a lot on his mind, and was having to deal with substantial criticism in certain places, as I've already mentioned.'

'From whom?' Whitney asked.

'Dr Angus McDonnell from Lenchester University was at the presentation on Sunday afternoon. There was an element of antagonism between the two of them.'

'Yes, we've already been informed about that. Would you say they had a difficult relationship?'

'Yes, they did.' He scratched his head, a perplexed look in his eyes. 'I couldn't quite get to the bottom of it. It seemed to go deeper than the actual theory. But when I broached the subject with Professor Hargrove, he told me it was nothing. He said that Angus McDonnell was, to quote him, a "jumped-up nobody" who was trying to hang on to his coat-tails.'

George audibly sucked in a breath, and Whitney turned to her. 'Is that an extreme view?'

'Not extreme, but certainly interesting,' George said.

Whitney nodded, deciding not to pursue the discussion until they were alone.

She leant forwards slightly, her eyes narrowing in thought as she processed Merchant's words. 'So is McDonnell a supporter of the Death's Shadow theory?' she asked, a hint of scepticism threading through her voice. Her gaze, sharp and assessing, lingered on Merchant, trying to read between the lines.

Merchant nodded. 'I believe so.'

Whitney's posture relaxed, but her mind was racing. 'Yet he wasn't backwards in coming forwards with his criticisms. Why's that?'

What was driving McDonnell's contradicting behaviours?

'It was because he didn't believe in all aspects of the theory, which is far-reaching,' Merchant explained.

Whitney's fingers tapped lightly on her leg. 'Did McDonnell want to be a part of the professor's team?'

Merchant shook his head. 'I doubt it because, according to Hargrove, there was some competitiveness there.'

Whitney nodded, her expression thoughtful. 'I see. And what about Dr Valerie Jenkins? Did the professor have anything to say about her?' She kept her voice steady, but internally, she was preparing for any significant revelation.

'Actually, yes. He moaned about her generally several times, but when I pushed him about it, he wouldn't elaborate.'

Merchant's reply piqued Whitney's interest further, her brow furrowing as she pondered the implications. 'Did you have a close relationship with the professor, would you say?' Her voice was calm, but internally she was keenly aware of the importance of the answer.

'Not really. He didn't have close relationships with anyone. Although I was his research assistant, he kept me at a distance.'

Merchant's response confirmed what Whitney had suspected, and she nodded slightly.

'I see. And is there anything else you can tell us about Professor Hargrove? Had he seemed ill recently?'

'No, he was his usual self. I wouldn't say he was the fittest of people – he seldom exercised – but he didn't seem sick.'

'Okay. Well, thank you for your time. You may return to the conference. But if you do think of anything, please let us know.'

Whitney was polite yet firm, her eyes conveying a sincere request for further cooperation. As Merchant prepared to leave, she remained seated, her mind already turning over the new information, pondering the next steps in her investigation.

Once he'd gone, Whitney turned to George, leaning back slightly as she pondered the relationship between Hargrove and his assistant.

'Was Merchant's relationship with Hargrove typical of a professor with their research assistant?'

George tucked a strand of hair behind her ear, a gesture that seemed to mirror Whitney's own thoughtful stance on the matter.

'I wouldn't say typical, but also not unusual.' Her voice was measured, but with an undercurrent of criticism. 'Hargrove was an arrogant academic who believed that he was always correct. He clearly used Merchant for his research skills, without giving him much credit.'

'Would that be sufficient for him to have murdered the professor?' Whitney's question cut through the air, direct and to the point.

'Judging by his body language, I'd say no.' George's hands gestured subtly as she spoke, emphasising her point. 'He appeared to accept our reason for questioning him, and didn't act as if he was trying to fool us into believing a certain scenario.'

'Okay, that's good to know.' Whitney checked her watch. 'I'm going back to the station. I'll return later, towards the end of the panel, so we can talk to Dr Jenkins. I'll ask Brian to come and pick me up.'

ELEVEN

I slide the vials of insulin from my bag and arrange them neatly in the drawer under the sink in the bathroom.

Fortunately, I had more than enough to carry out my plan.

All thanks to those health service workers who believe they know better than me how to control my diabetes. They insist I need more insulin than I do.

Idiots.

I played along, being the ever compliant patient.

That doesn't mean it's not bloody infuriating when they act so superior just because my readings are off one day. They don't see the whole picture. My levels spike at night but even out by morning. I know how to care for myself. Nothing's more aggravating than some patronising nurse thinking they know what's best for me.

As if they have any idea what I've been through.

But now it's paid off. I have enough insulin to do as I please.

And what I please is to end the life of anyone who gets in my way.

Let's take the pompous, arrogant Professor Jonathan Hargrove... Now deceased.

He brought his untimely end on himself. We could have worked together on the theory, considering we were both heading in the same direction.

But no.

That arse-wipe thought he could ride roughshod over me.

When I approached him months ago, he dismissed me out of hand, like I was nothing more than an insignificant annoyance.

Well, I bet he'd like a second chance now, given the opportunity.

Because this 'nobody' got the better of him. And all he could do was stare at me in shock whilst the insulin did its work.

I'd thought about recording his demise on my phone, then decided against it. There's no incriminating evidence anywhere. And it needs to stay that way.

I close the bathroom drawer and glance up at the flickering fluorescent light, which is buzzing faintly. I complained about it yesterday, but has anyone come to fix it?

Of course not.

I bet they'd be here like a shot if I was one of their esteemed presenters. One of their top-notch researchers.

I shrug. I'm not prepared to get annoyed about it, because I'll be up there with the best of them soon.

When I present my previously unpublished work, they'll forget all about Hargrove.

I'll get the credit, the admiration and accolades.

It's me who's going to be regarded as the psychologist who revolutionised our understanding of serial killers.

And do you know why it's going to be me?

It's obvious, isn't it?

You have to live close to a killer to truly comprehend their dark, twisted mind.

No one knows that like I do.

But we'll keep that little secret between us.

No one knows who I am.

Not since I changed my name and disappeared after the sordid truth emerged.

I digress...

My point is, you need first-hand experience inside that darkness to truly understand it, not some Oxbridge navel-gazing and guesswork.

And what's with calling the theory Death's Shadow? A lurid, sensationalist title meant to grab attention for what should have been a seminal theory revealing the inner workings of the serial-killing mind.

But soon, Hargrove's shadow will fade.

I'll bide my time through this tedious conference, suffering the sycophants fawning over his memory. Once he's gone from everyone's mind, I'll step into the light where I belong.

Everyone will know my name. My work.

This theory is mine. And mine alone.

TWELVE

Wednesday

George stood at the side of the stage in the large conference room, her presence almost blending into the shadows cast by the dim lighting. She observed the panel's set-up; it had generated such buzz that it was moved to the largest room to accommodate the expected crowd of over a hundred attendees. As she watched, the seats filled steadily, the hum of eager conversations vibrating through the air.

The panel consisted of five individuals, including herself, standing in for Jonathan Hargrove. Her fellow panellist Dr Valerie Jenkins, who they intended to confer with later regarding Hargrove, was an expert in serial killing throughout the ages. The other three on the panel were: Dr Henri Rousseau, a distinguished French criminologist; Professor Gwendolyn Dixon, a leading forensic scientist from Wales; and Dr Samuel Thompson from the United States, a renowned expert in serial crime investigation. Each of them shared a fascination in the psyche of serial killers.

Briefed earlier, George knew the format was simple yet

open-ended – introductions followed by an interactive session with the audience on the topic of serial killers. The thought of the impending discussions sent a trickle of anticipation through her. Last night she'd read up on each panellist.

Dr Jenkins was the only one who hadn't yet made an appearance, the others having already taken their places on the stage. George lingered in the wings, her intent gaze scanning the incoming attendees. She was searching for something – anything – that might manifest as a clue in their demeanour: a hidden twitch or a furtive glance that could betray a suspect among them. Someone who was responsible for the death of Hargrove.

Her attention was suddenly drawn to a door that had swung open at the side of the room. It was seldom used except by the conference staff. Through it stepped one of the organisers, her face taut with urgency. George's eyes narrowed as she watched her exchange a hushed conversation with the panel's moderator. The air between them was thick with unspoken alarm and their body language spoke volumes – shock, dropped jaws, a frenetic undercurrent of panic.

Curiosity piqued and a tingle of concern knotting her stomach, George hurried over to them. 'I'm Dr Cavendish on the panel, as you probably know,' she interjected, keeping her voice calm as she addressed the visibly rattled organisers. 'Is there a problem?'

The organisers shared a loaded glance, their hesitation tangible as their eyes flicked to her and away, as if struggling with the weight of their news.

George's instincts, honed from years of police work with Whitney, screamed that this was more than a simple hiccup in the day's schedule.

'I work with the police, and I'm here in that capacity as well, investigating the untimely demise of Professor Hargrove. If there's something amiss, I need to know immediately.' Her voice was firm, implying it was not up for discussion.

A pause stretched between them, laden with reluctance. Then the organiser seemed to muster the courage to answer. She turned to George. 'Dr Valerie Jenkins is dead in her room.'

The words hit George like a physical blow. Not another death. Her mind raced, a whirlwind of implications and questions. 'Was it you who found her?'

'Yes.' The woman nodded.

'Okay, what have you done so far?' George demanded in a steady voice.

'I've alerted reception, and they're calling the paramedics as we speak,' came the shaky reply.

'Has anyone been to the room since the body was discovered?'

'I don't know. No, no, I don't think so. I came straight here after calling for an ambulance.'

'Quickly, walk me through what happened,' George urged, her mind meticulously constructing a timeline and the next steps.

'I went to Dr Jenkins' room to see if she was there because she hadn't turned up for the panel.' The organiser's voice trembled as she began. 'I found her lying on the bed.'

'How did you get into the room?'

'The door was ajar so I walked in. Everything was eerily still. At first, I thought she might be sleeping, but she looked... off.'

George's attention sharpened. 'How did you confirm she wasn't asleep?'

'I called out to her, but there was no response. Then I got closer and saw her eyes were open, staring vacantly at the ceiling. That's when I panicked and checked for a pulse,' the organiser explained, her voice still shaky.

'And you found none?' George pressed, seeking clarity.

'No. Her skin was cold, and she wasn't breathing. Then I knew for sure. I... I can't believe it.'

'Did you touch anything else in the room after that?' George asked, hoping the integrity of the scene was maintained.

'No. I phoned down to reception to ask for an ambulance and then came here.'

'We need to secure the scene immediately,' she stated with urgency, already moving towards the door.

As the conference organiser hurried alongside her, George's thoughts were a step ahead, piecing together the fragments of a mystery that had just deepened, the shadows of the conference room mirroring the dark turn of events.

'So nobody else knows, only those on reception, right?' George confirmed, her words clipped.

'That's correct.'

'I want it kept that way. Suspend the panel for now.' Her gaze swept across the bewildered conference attendees who were already fidgeting in their seats because it hadn't started. 'Don't inform the delegates of the reason, just say that we're hoping to start again later.' She was planning ahead, already strategising the best way to control the situation. 'I don't want anyone to leave. Understand? And no mention of what's happened to anyone.' It was crucial to keep the circle of knowledge tight for now.

'Yes, okay.'

'What room was Jenkins in?' George asked.

'Third floor. Room 311.'

'Okay. I'll be informing the police to let them know what's happening.'

At reception, George caught the receptionist's eye. 'I've been informed about Dr Valerie Jenkins. I'm going upstairs to the room. Make sure no one else comes up until the paramedics arrive. Understood?' She didn't wait for a response, her authoritative command was enough to convey the gravity of the situation.

George left reception and made her way to the conference accommodation, pressing the button for the lift with more force than necessary. Her mind whirred with possibilities and consequences, the weight of another death heavy on her shoulders.

Upon reaching the third floor, she found the room's door slightly open. She went inside. It was silent apart from the hum of the fluorescent light. Jenkins was lying on her bed, her eyes fixed on the ceiling in a vacant stare. There was something terribly final in that stillness, a silence that screamed.

George took a quick look around the room. No immediate signs of a struggle. The neatness of the room was at odds with the tragedy it contained. She took out her phone and called Whitney, who answered almost before the first ring had finished.

'I know, the panel starts soon – I'm on my wa—' Whitney replied.

'It's not that, Whitney,' George interrupted, her voice calm, despite her mind churning with the implications of what this death meant. 'You do need to get here. But don't go to the conference room; instead, come to room 311. Valerie Jenkins has been found dead. It looks like similar circumstances to Jonathan Hargrove.'

The pregnant pause on the other end of the line hung in the air. 'You've got to be kidding, right?'

'No, I'm not.'

'Okay, I'll be with you as soon as possible, and I'll let Claire know.'

'The paramedics have been called. I'll wait for them in the room rather than reception where more people might work out what's going on.' George paced, her eyes inadvertently drawn to Valerie's still form. 'It'll cause too much attention. I'll let them know that it's been taken over as a police investigation.'

After the briefest of goodbyes, George ended the call, her attention snapping to the door as the paramedics arrived.

'Good afternoon. I'm Dr Georgina Cavendish. I'm working with Lenchester Police.' Her introduction was cut and dry. 'We suspect this is a suspicious death, and your presence isn't yet needed.' She eyed the paramedics, their kits ready for use.

'Do you have any ID?' one paramedic, clearly taken aback, asked.

George's patience thinned. 'I've already informed you who I am.' Her manner was sharp, like a teacher reprimanding a student. 'If you require any further information, then I suggest you speak to them at reception.'

'We need to verify the death,' the paramedic insisted.

'Fine, please put on gloves.'

'Already on,' he replied, showing his hands.

George took a second to notice the clear gloves – different from the usual blue – before refocusing on the task at hand.

'Fine. You may ascertain that she's dead. Do not move her.' George hovered close, her eyes hawk-like as the paramedic headed towards the body.

'Yes, the patient is deceased,' the paramedic confirmed to his colleague.

'Right. Please leave now. No one is to be in the room until the police and the pathologist arrive.'

As the paramedics departed, George scanned the room methodically. The victim's stunned expression was frozen, secrets locked inside. What led to the woman's death and how was it connected to Hargrove's?

THIRTEEN

Wednesday

Whitney stared at the phone in her hand, her heart racing a stark rhythm against the eerie silence of her office. 'Not another one,' she murmured to herself, the words tasting bitter in her mouth. The timing was catastrophic. With George's wedding just over a week away, the shadow of a potential serial killer loomed ominously over their plans.

As the lead detective, she couldn't let personal events interfere, but the thought gnawed at her. How could they celebrate knowing there was a killer on the loose? George and Ross didn't deserve this dark cloud over their special day.

Not only that, the implications of a second death were dire. They had to catch the killer before the conference's conclusion. If they didn't, it would make their job much harder and... Whitney's thoughts trailed off, unwilling to finish the sentence even in her own head.

She had to alert her team and formulate a plan of action. But first, she needed to inform the super. Her hand was steady as she dialled the internal phone, but her pulse betrayed her anxiety.

The phone clicked, and her boss's voice cut through the tension. 'Superintendent Clyde.'

'Hello, ma'am, it's Whitney,' she began, her voice a mix of urgency and composure. 'I thought I'd give you a call before I went out. You won't have heard yet, but we have another death at the criminology conference. Dr Cavendish is there at the moment, and she's taken over supervision of the scene to make sure it doesn't get contaminated.'

'Who's dead?'

'Dr Valerie Jenkins. We'd actually earmarked her for interview following the panel because of her link with Professor Hargrove.'

'Any ideas on the cause of death?'

'Nothing official yet because the pathologist hasn't arrived, but Dr Cavendish believes it's similar circumstances to Hargrove. The woman was found lying on her bed with no outward signs of struggle or cause of death.'

'I'll have to let Chief Superintendent Douglas know.'

Whitney's hand subconsciously gripped the phone tighter at the mention of her archnemesis Dickhead Douglas – as she'd nicknamed him. He'd been on her case for years, ever since she was a lowly police constable. Despite Clyde's supportive presence, acting as a buffer between the two of them, the thought of dealing with Douglas again was like having a stone in her stomach.

'Does he need to know yet?' Whitney questioned, which she hoped didn't sound too much like a whine. Surely Douglas's involvement could be postponed, if not altogether avoided.

'Yes, he does.' The response from Clyde was a resigned agreement – a shared understanding.

'Okay, ma'am.' She stood up, the motion a physical preparation for the tasks ahead. 'I'm off to brief the team, and then will go to the crime scene. I'd rather we still hung back from having a press conference. Let's keep it contained until we know more about what we're dealing with.'

'For now, I agree, but we can't wait for too long. The news vultures will be circling soon because we won't be able to keep the deaths quiet for long. It's better that we control the narrative,' Clyde stated.

'I agree, ma'am. After I've visited the scene we can think again.'

'Okay, keep me informed, Whitney.' Clyde's words were a tether, a reminder that she wasn't alone in this.

Whitney replaced the phone back on its cradle with a deliberate gentleness that belied the turmoil inside her. Her hand hovered for a moment, as if to ensure the conversation was truly confined to the past. Then, snatching up her bag and shrugging into her jacket with brisk efficiency, she made her way through the door that led into the incident room. Her steps were even, her spine straight, forcing the outward signs of control she felt beginning to slip.

'Listen up, everyone. We have trouble,' she announced. Her gaze swept over her team, each face reflecting concern, curiosity, or concentration. She picked up a marker, her fingers wrapping around it a touch too tightly, betraying her stress to any observant eye. 'I've just heard from George. We have another suspicious death at the conference.'

'You've got to be kidding,' Frank said, leaning back in his chair, his arms crossing over his chest in a defensive posture that mirrored Whitney's internal resistance to the news.

'No, I'm not,' she replied, her jaw tightening. 'I'm about to go to the scene. Brian, call the pathology department. Ask them to send someone out there. Make sure it's Claire.'

Brian's brows furrowed, a clear sign of his reluctance. 'I don't think I can dictate who goes,' he countered, his uncertainty a sharp contrast to Whitney's resolve.

'Just try,' she insisted, her fingers drumming an impatient rhythm on the side of the marker. 'We don't want anyone else. Claire was at the other scene. We need the continuity. Use that as the reasoning.'

'Well, providing she's on duty...' Brian's voice trailed, the sentence unfinished, much like the many threads of the investigation that occupied Whitney's thoughts.

'Just do it, please, Brian,' she said, her words sounding more like a command than a request. She was all too aware of how thin her patience was stretched, like a wire pulled taut.

'Right, our murder victim is Dr Valerie Jenkins.' Whitney's hand was steady as she turned and wrote the name on the board, the marker squeaking with every letter punctuating her rising anxiety.

'But she was the person we suspected could have been involved in Hargrove's murder,' Doug interjected, his forehead creased in thought.

'That's correct. Clearly, she wasn't,' Whitney retorted, her words clipped, as if cutting off that line of enquiry.

'Well, not necessarily,' Frank chimed in, his tone sceptical, his body leaning forward. 'How do we know it's not a murder and then a suicide? Maybe Jenkins realised we were on to her and took her own life,' he suggested.

'Too convenient, Frank. Too clean,' she mused.

'You don't know that, guv,' Frank said.

'Okay, I accept that we shouldn't make any assumptions. All we know for now is that Hargrove is dead, and so too is Jenkins. As yet, we don't know if it's a suspicious death. We'll know that from Claire, but we have to assume that it is. Now, is there anything I need to know before leaving for the conference centre?' she asked.

Silence ensued, the team reflecting her own unease – the quiet before the storm.

'Hang on a minute,' Ellie called out, her head emerging

from behind her monitor. 'I've just heard back from Mac in Forensics regarding Hargrove's laptop.'

'And?' Whitney pressed, her fingers stopping their tapping to grip the edge of the whiteboard.

'Give me a second. I haven't yet opened the email.' Ellie's voice betrayed a slight tremor of excitement, or perhaps apprehension.

Whitney's nerves vibrated with a thread of impatience. She needed facts, evidence, leads – not delays. She could almost hear the clock ticking, each second another moment lost, another advantage given to the killer.

'Come on, Ellie, don't keep us all hanging in suspense,' Frank said, echoing Whitney's urgency.

'On the laptop, I can see here some heated emails between Professor Hargrove and Dr McDonnell,' Ellie reported, her voice increasing in volume with the implication of this find.

'What do they say?' Whitney demanded, anxious to hear.

'There's one from Hargrove telling McDonnell to stop trying to discredit his theory, or he will make sure that the academic community is aware of what he did when they were at Oxford,' Ellie explained, scrolling through the emails with a furrowed brow.

'What did he do?' Whitney probed, her mind racing through possibilities, each more incriminating than the last.

'It doesn't say,' Ellie said.

Whitney's frustration mounted. 'Did McDonnell reply?'

'Yes. McDonnell said that Hargrove had no proof and that he'd do whatever it took to show that Hargrove's work wasn't what he claimed it to be.'

'Did Hargrove respond?' Whitney demanded.

'Yes. It was short. He just said, "I'm warning you – back off, or it'll be the end of your career".'

Whitney stood back, the implications crashing into her like waves. 'McDonnell is deeper into this than we first thought.'

Her fingers curled into a fist. 'Okay, right, we've got something now. A much stronger link between Hargrove and McDonnell – a lot more than McDonnell told us when we interviewed him,' she concluded, the marker tapping against the whiteboard in a staccato rhythm that matched her quickening pulse.

'Do you think this is linked to the text messages Jenkins had with Hargrove that were on his phone?' Brian asked.

'Maybe. We don't yet know. Ellie, I want you to dig into McDonnell and Jenkins. Let's find out if there's a link between them and whether or not we can bring together all three of them,' Whitney instructed, turning her penetrating gaze on the younger officer, who nodded, her fingers already dancing over the keyboard. 'And the rest of you,' Whitney continued, her voice rising to command the room, 'carry on with what you're doing. Look into Hargrove and McDonnell more generally. Check CCTV, and let's see if Jenkins was anywhere near Hargrove's room during the time of his murder.'

'We could do with more up-to-date CCTV footage, guv,' Frank said.

'I'll ask them to forward it to you. Brian and Meena, I want you to investigate the finances of McDonnell, Hargrove, and Jenkins. Let's see if there's any indication of blackmail, or if any money has changed hands. There's something tying them together and we need to discover what it is. Check social media, too, for all three of them. As two are dead and only McDonnell is left, my bet is that either he's next, or he's our killer. I'm off to the conference centre. You know where I am if you need me,' she said, her words final.

Before leaving, Whitney looked around the room, her eyes locking with each member of her team, imparting the gravity of their task. She could feel the team's energy aligning with her own, their movements becoming more purposeful, more driven. The urgency was tangible, galvanising them into action.

FOURTEEN

Wednesday

Whitney pulled into the car park, the gravel crunching under her tyres – a mundane sound that felt oddly soothing given the chaos of the day. She passed through the entrance of the conference centre, her steps measured and silent on the polished floor. At the reception desk was a familiar face, a small comfort in the storm of the case.

'Wayne, we need more CCTV footage from the conference centre and also in the accommodation. Send it to the usual address. I want everything from yesterday and today, until as late as possible,' Whitney instructed.

Wayne nodded and tapped quickly at the keyboard. 'Yes, I'll get on to it straight away,' he responded with efficiency.

Whitney's gaze flicked to the clock on the wall, noting the time – two-thirty. 'At least until two this afternoon, if possible.'

'I'll do it now.'

'Thanks. Where's Valerie Jenkins' room?'

'Third floor, 311. Turn right as you step out of the elevator.'

'Thanks,' she said, biting her tongue at him not using the word *lift*.

When her dad was alive, he'd go on at length at the way British English was being infiltrated with American English. He was passionate about it. Elevator – lift; trash – rubbish. He'd turn in his grave if he knew that *gotten* was becoming prevalent among younger people.

With the directions given, she found herself waiting for the lift, the metallic doors reflecting her steeled determination. Once inside, her image stared back at her in the mirror walls – a mixture of resolve and weariness. The door slid open with a ding, and she stepped out onto the third floor. She followed the numbered plaques until she stood before the door to Valerie Jenkins' room. George was standing in the entrance, a silent sentinel.

'You're here. Good,' George said.

'Let's have a look, then.' Whitney pushed the door fully open with a sense of foreboding.

One look at the body, and her detective instincts surged. 'I agree, it's exactly the same as Hargrove.' Her voice was steady, but her mind raced – patterns were emerging, ones she couldn't yet decipher.

George turned from the window, where she'd been gazing out pensively. 'Yes, with the exception that Jenkins' eyes are open, whereas Hargrove's were closed.'

A memory tugged at Whitney's consciousness, and she frowned. 'How do we know that?'

'From speaking to Emily Davies, if you remember. She said that it looked like Hargrove was asleep.'

Whitney's internal frustration at the oversight showed itself in a brief, annoyed tap of her foot. 'Oh yes, I forgot.' Her hands slipped into latex gloves with practised ease. 'Have you searched the room?' Her eyes swept the room, absorbing every detail – the position of the curtains, the placement of the luggage, a glass sitting on a coaster.

'No, I was waiting for you, because I had no gloves. Also, I wanted to make sure that no one tried to enter, so I stood close to the door after the paramedics had left,' George explained, her posture stiff with the responsibility she'd shouldered.

'Okay,' she said, handing George some gloves. 'Bathroom first.'

They walked into the room, where the mundane items of daily life – shampoo, conditioner, shower gel – were laid out with an orderliness that seemed at odds with what had occurred in the room next door. Whitney's hand passed over the assortment of toiletries, feeling the familiar adrenaline that came with the hunt for evidence. She reached for the bag tucked under the sink, her movements deliberate, almost reverent.

'Nothing in here of any interest. Do we know how old the woman is? She looks to be in her fifties, but doesn't appear to be taking any medicines. There aren't even any supplements in here. That's really weird,' she said, her mind ticking over the implications.

'Not everyone has to be on medication, Whitney,' George observed, her tone light but her eyes serious.

'True, but most people take something,' Whitney countered. 'Unless the killer removed whatever it was that Jenkins was taking, because it was incriminating.'

'Is that likely, if she'd been given insulin, like Hargrove?' George asked.

'Your guess is as good as mine. Let's take a look around the bedroom.' Whitney's voice carried a mix of command and anticipation. 'We need her laptop. I have a feeling that will give us some answers. Did you check whether it's there?'

'I didn't look for it specifically, but nothing's been touched, so if it's here, we'll find it,' George said as they left the bathroom.

Whitney glanced towards the corner where the woman's handbag, a black leather tote, was placed on a chair. Approaching it methodically, her fingers brushed over the surface before delving inside. A mobile was close to the top. 'We'll take this,' she said, placing it into an evidence bag with deliberate care.

'I can't see a laptop here,' George said as she paced around the room.

'Damn. I bet the killer took it. Is there anything else of use?' Whitney's brows furrowed as she crouched down, peering under the bed. Finding nothing, she straightened up, her attention focusing on the wardrobe. 'Try the wardrobe,' she instructed.

George moved towards it and opened the door with a gentle pull. 'There are a few clothes hanging – enough here for the conference. That's all. Where's her suitcase?'

'It's under the window,' Whitney said, spotting it.

George turned to investigate, rummaging through the small piece of luggage. 'All that's in here is underwear, nothing else.'

'What about her conference papers?' Whitney asked.

'Her conference folder's on the table over there,' George replied, moving towards the mentioned item. She picked up the folder and browsed through it. 'She's written a few notes…' Her voice trailed off.

'What is it?' Whitney approached, focusing on the folder in her friend's hand.

George held out the folder for Whitney to see. 'She clearly was at the Sunday talk by Hargrove. She's written *Sunday* and then she's scribbled a few criticisms, but not much detail.'

Whitney read the scribbles and gave a low chuckle. 'So that's how academics do their critiques, is it? She's written *idiot* on more than one occasion, plus *not proved* and *contentious*.'

'Yes, it does seems like she was simply jotting down odd thoughts that came into her mind during the presentation.'

'We'll take her papers with us,' Whitney decided with a decisive nod, handing George an evidence bag, whilst filing away each detail in her mental catalogue of evidence.

Whitney paused for a moment, allowing herself to observe Jenkins. The woman lay there, her life cut short. A tragic victim. 'I wonder if the murderer actually placed her at that angle, because she's not actually straight.'

'She could have moved slightly if the killer left before the woman was actually dead,' George suggested.

'Good point,' Whitney mused. 'What's that?' she suddenly said, distracted by something peeking out from under the pillow. She stepped towards the bed. 'It's a notebook, I think.' A surge of adrenaline sharpened her focus as she gently extracted it. Her hands were steady even though her heart raced with the possibility of new revelations. 'I reckon we've got something,' Whitney breathed out, a spark of victory in her voice as she considered the notebook's placement. 'The murderer clearly couldn't have seen this, because it was under the victim's pillow. That confirms the victim must have moved slightly afterwards or I wouldn't have spotted it.'

'What's in it?' George asked, moving towards Whitney and peering over her shoulder.

Whitney leafed through the pages. 'Look,' she said, pointing at one of the pages, her voice a mix of triumph and gravity. 'Notes about Hargrove. Nothing like what was written on her conference notes. These are far more detailed. Here she's writing about the theory, and look at this – Angus McDonnell's name is mentioned. This is interesting... Jenkins and McDonnell working together, do you think?'

George leant in further with an expression of intrigue. 'Oh, I see...'

'What?' Whitney asked impatiently.

'This is more like an academic journal. There are the notes discussing their own theory – but not what it is exactly – and yes, you're right, they do appear to be working together. The implication here is that Jenkins and McDonnell's theory can be used to discredit Hargrove, and then theirs will be the one to take the limelight. Very interesting.'

Whitney's fingers hovered over the notebook and her eyes flicked up to George, gauging her reaction. 'What do you think their theory is?'

Her colleague's face was etched with contemplation. 'Maybe they're building on Hargrove's work, or they've suggested something entirely new. Whatever it is, it needs investigating. It could prove to be the motive for the murders.'

'But that makes no sense. Hargrove and Jenkins appear to be on opposite sides,' Whitney pondered out loud, her brows knitting together in thought. The room seemed to close in around them as the weight of the question settled. 'We'll worry about that later. Let's take this notebook with us because it's certainly evidence of some description, or Jenkins wouldn't have kept it hidden.'

George nodded, watching her carefully. 'Agreed.'

'We'd better wait for Claire to come before calling Forensics, because she'll want to be here first.' Whitney glanced at her watch. 'Hopefully she should be here soon. Actually, is that Claire?' She looked towards the door as the sound of approaching footsteps grew louder.

Whitney closed the notebook and tucked it securely into an evidence bag. Her mind was a whirlwind of questions and theories, each vying for her attention. As she stood there, the end of the bed forming a barrier between her and the lifeless form of Jenkins, she couldn't help but feel a twinge of sorrow for the woman whose life had ended in such dire circumstances.

FIFTEEN

Wednesday

The door opened and Claire marched in, her white coat billowing behind her like a cape caught in a gust of wind. 'Right, everyone step back,' the pathologist demanded theatrically, her voice cutting through the tension in the room like a scalpel. There was a palpable sense of urgency in her movements, a professional briskness that commanded attention.

George observed Claire with a pensive gaze. She knew her well enough to see the telltale signs of strain. That was the trouble with all the cuts services were having to deal with; everyone was overworked.

'Oh, thank goodness it's you, Claire,' Whitney expressed with evident relief, her shoulders sagging slightly as if shedding the weight of worry. 'I was worried someone else might be on duty.'

'It's always me,' Claire said, the corners of her mouth turning upwards in a smile that was more of a well-rehearsed gesture than an expression of amusement. 'At least, it always seems to be whenever there's a murder. It's like there's some sort of agreement among murderers: "Make sure Claire's on duty before you kill."' She snorted, her ironic humour a light relief in the grimness of their surroundings.

Whitney frowned. 'But investigating suspicious deaths is your job, so of course you'll be called out.'

'All I meant was that murders happen more often when I'm on duty than when others in my department are.'

'Well, I'm glad they do because you're the best, Claire, and you can't deny it,' Whitney said, with a grin.

'I didn't say I was going to. I'm not that foolish,' Claire responded, her posture stiffening. 'Right, what have we got? I don't have time for chit-chat.'

'It looks to me like the same as Hargrove, so I imagine we could be looking at insulin overdose,' Whitney said, stepping closer to the body, her gaze never leaving the pale, still face of the victim.

Claire's eyebrow arched in a silent but potent challenge. 'Oh, right. Congratulations, Whitney.' The pathologist's voice dripped with irony.

'On what?' Whitney's brows furrowed in confusion.

'On passing all your exams to become a pathologist, because clearly, you no longer need my input.' The smirk on Claire's lips was thin, almost cutting. 'And where, may I ask, did you do the testing to discover it was insulin?' Claire's sarcasm was like a sharpened blade.

George stared at the pathologist. Claire valued her territory, her expertise, and Whitney's leap to conclusions, however well-intentioned, was encroaching on that. But even George realised that Claire had overreacted.

Whitney sighed, a soft exhalation of frustration. 'I was just making an assumption, Claire. There's no need for you to speak to me like that.' She stood her ground, meeting the pathologist's eyes with an admirable steadiness.

Claire's expression shifted, betraying a moment of vulnerability that she quickly masked. 'You're right, I'm sorry. It was wrong of me to snap.' Her voice, now softer, carried a hint of genuine remorse.

George exchanged a glance with Whitney; the brief flicker of concern was unmistakable between them. Claire was seldom apologetic, a trait as dependable as her professional rigour.

'Is everything okay, Claire?' Whitney ventured, sounding concerned. 'You're not acting at all like your normal self.'

George agreed with her friend. She'd seen Claire in many states, but today there was an edge to her that was most unfamiliar.

'I'm not prepared to discuss it now. I'm at work,' Claire replied, deflecting with the professionalism they were accustomed to, but her voice had a brittle quality, like thin ice over a deep lake.

'Is anything wrong with Ralph?' Whitney probed further, appearing unwilling to let the anomaly pass without comment.

'Whitney, I'm not prepared to discuss it,' Claire said, glaring at them.

'Yes, but maybe we should go out for a drink later and we can have a chat if you like?' Whitney offered, extending an olive branch.

Claire's jaw tightened, a clear sign of her escalating tension.

'For the third and final time, drop it.' Claire's voice was firm, leaving no room for further enquiry.

'Okay, sorry,' Whitney conceded, raising her hand in a gesture of peace. 'You get on. By the way, there was a notebook sticking out from under the pillow, which I did pull out and put into an evidence bag, but didn't touch the body.'

Claire's eyes narrowed slightly, but her nod indicated she understood. 'You'd better not have done,' she said with a mix of jest and seriousness as she pulled out her camera and began to circle the body with the practised grace of a seasoned professional.

Whitney and George stepped back, giving Claire room to work.

George's mind raced with possibilities. What secrets did the notebook hold? How did it tie into the murder? She could almost feel the answers brushing against the edge of her understanding, like leaves in the wind, just out of reach.

'I assume you've taken a look around,' Claire said as she changed lenses on her camera for a closer shot.

Whitney nodded, her arms crossed. 'Yes, and there was no medication. Absolutely none. Not even a supplement, which struck me as odd for someone of her age. Toiletries are all there, but nothing else. There's no laptop, either. I took a phone from the handbag, and we've taken the notebook because there's quite a lot of incriminating information in there.'

Claire lowered her camera and looked over at them. 'I need to get the body back to the morgue and will test for insulin immediately.'

A chill coursed through George at the mention of insulin again. It would be a troubling pattern, a murderer using such a specific and silent method to claim their victims. The notebook could indeed hold vital clues; its contents might reveal a motive buried in academic rivalry or something more sinister.

Whitney caught George's eye. 'Once Claire has finished her initial examination, we should go through the notebook in detail. Every word could be a potential lead.'

George nodded in agreement. 'Absolutely. I have a feeling we're only scratching the surface with what we've read so far.'

They watched as Claire continued her work before packing away her kit.

'Right, can we get Forensics in here now?' Whitney asked, when it was clear that Claire had finished. 'We need them to go through the room once the body has been taken away.'

'You may.' Claire gave her permission.

'Thanks. We're going to go back to the station now,'

DEATH'S SHADOW

Whitney said, rubbing the back of her neck in a habitual gesture of frustration.

'Well, I can't,' George said. 'There's the panel. If we're going to let the conference continue, then the panel needs to go ahead. They've already had to wait forty-five minutes for it to start.'

'Yes, I forgot. You go to the panel and, Claire, we'll see you soon. Let me know whenever you have anything to tell us. And, look, I mean it – if you want to chat anytime...' Whitney trailed off, her concern for Claire almost tangible as she gestured vaguely with her hands, as if trying to physically offer her support.

'Thank you, Whitney, but for now, it's fine. I can deal with my issues,' Claire replied curtly, but her hands betrayed a slight tremor as she turned away to busy herself with her professional duties.

Whitney and George walked out and went over to the lift. 'You and Claire, like peas in a pod,' Whitney said with a slight smirk, as if trying to inject some lightness into the heavy atmosphere.

'What on earth do you mean?' George asked, not understanding Whitney's teasing. She crossed her arms, as if to ward off the emotional probe she sensed was coming.

'You're alike. You keep everything to yourself, all this stiff-upper-lip and not-sharing nonsense. Like being vulnerable is a sign of weakness,' Whitney observed, her head tilted to the side, as if she was analysing George.

'It's not like that, Whitney, but we're not all like you,' George replied, her voice carrying a defensive edge. She shifted her weight from one foot to the other, uncomfortable with where the conversation was heading.

'Yes, I get it. I wear my heart on my sleeve, and everything affects me, but having said that, I know sometimes it's best to talk about things. Like, you know, is everything okay with you and Ross?' Whitney prodded, her eyes softening, filled with a genuine concern.

'Yes, we're fine. Or at least we will be after the wedding. You don't need to ask me about that. After the panel, I'm going home because we have more wedding stuff to sort out,' George said.

'That's fine. I'll see you at the station tomorrow,' Whitney said just as her phone rang. She pulled it out of her pocket. 'Hold on, I'd better get this – it's from Mum's care home.' Her expression shifted to one of concern. 'Hello, Whitney speaking.'

George watched as Whitney's features paled, a knot forming in her stomach. By the expression on her friend's face, something was amiss. Whitney's mother had dementia. Was it linked to that?

'Okay, I'll get there as soon as I can,' Whitney said, ending the call. She turned to George, her eyes wide with worry. 'It's Mum.'

'What's happened?' George enquired, her voice laced with sympathy.

'I'm not sure. They didn't explain exactly, other than to ask me to go in to see them because there are some issues. I'm going now. I'll contact the team and tell them where I am. I'll see you tomorrow morning,' Whitney said, her speech quickening with her rising anxiety.

'Is there anything I can do? Would you like me to go with you?' George offered.

'No, it's fine. I know Rob was meant to be seeing her tomorrow,' Whitney said, a subtle shake in her voice as she referred to her older brother, who was in assisted living because he had brain damage, from when attacked as a teenager. The weight of Whitney's family responsibilities appeared to be bearing down on her. 'I have to get in touch with him too. You go to the panel. Keep a note of anything untoward you notice.'

'What should I say if asked about Jenkins?'

'Act like you don't know. If the subject comes up, say you're unaware of what's happened. I'm sure some people will already know she's died by now, but you're not a police officer. You know nothing.'

George nodded. 'I hope everything's okay with your mother. I'm around all evening, so call me later if you'd like to talk about it,' she added, the offer hanging between them, laden with unspoken support.

'Yeah, thanks. I appreciate it,' Whitney said with a brief, grateful smile. 'Okay, right – I think I'll take the stairs. This lift seems to be taking forever,' Whitney said, her impatience with the delay evident as she quickly turned and started for the stairwell.

Her friend's rapid departure left George alone in the quiet corridor. She stood there for a moment, watching the space where Whitney had vanished, the sound of her hastening footsteps fading.

The lift arrived and as the doors opened she exhaled slowly, the sound almost lost in the hush of the empty hallway. Stepping inside and shifting her attention back to the task at hand, she mentally prepared herself for the panel and the potential questions that might be asked regarding the deaths of both Hargrove and Jenkins.

SIXTEEN

Wednesday

Whitney parked her car outside the front of Cumberland Court, the care home where her mum now lived and had done for the last couple of years. Even though it was certainly the best place for her, because she was no longer able to look after herself independently – and with Whitney's job and also having Tiffany and Ava living with her, it would be absolutely impossible for it to be otherwise – Whitney still felt guilty about her mum having to be there.

It wasn't that the staff treated her badly – they were wonderful, and Whitney couldn't have wished for a better, more caring place for her mum to be – but she still felt she was neglecting her duty. It was the same with her brother, Rob, even though he was actually thriving in the assisted-living home where he'd been living since their mum went into care, and was now able to do a lot of things for himself that he had previously struggled with.

Although sometimes there were horror stories in the media about what went on in care homes, Whitney believed that they were the exception. Obviously, otherwise, they wouldn't make the news.

Her feet crunched on the gravel as she made her way to the front door and walked inside. She approached the reception desk where Angela, who had been at the home for over ten years and was one of Whitney's favourite carers, was sitting. Another good thing about this particular home was that most of the staff had been there for years and seldom were agency staff called in. They all appeared to be happy in their work, and it meant that there was a good continuity of care. She couldn't have asked for more.

'Hello, Whitney,' Angela said, glancing up, a sympathetic look on her face. 'Sorry we had to call you in, but Lorraine wants to speak to you in person about your mum. Under the circumstances, she thought it would be best,' the carer said, referring to the manager of the home. 'She's in her office.'

'Okay, I'll go there first, thanks. Where's Mum at the moment?'

Angela couldn't meet her eyes. 'Lorraine will explain everything.'

Whitney swallowed hard. It couldn't be good if Angela wouldn't tell her what the issue was. She hurried around the side of the reception desk and along a short corridor before knocking on the manager's door.

'Come in,' a cheery woman's voice answered.

Whitney opened the door and went inside. Lorraine was seated behind her desk, an open laptop in front of her. She was in her late forties and had highlighted blonde hair, which was pulled back with a deep red headband. Unlike other members of staff, she didn't wear a uniform.

'You wanted to see me?' Whitney said, trying to force a smile, but failing.

Lorraine smiled, but it was tinged with sympathy. 'Yes,

Whitney, please come in and take a seat. I'm sorry to have to drag you away from work, but this wouldn't wait.'

'Okay,' Whitney said, closing the door behind her and heading over to one of the easy chairs opposite the desk. She didn't think the manager did it intentionally, but it did put Whitney at a bit of a disadvantage because she was in a lower position.

'Your mum's had a bit of a turn,' Lorraine said, gently.

Not again. Whitney's heart sank, a knot forming in her stomach.

'What do you mean by that?' Her voice was steadier than she felt, masking the surge of anxiety.

'Well, it happened after she had a fall this morning—'

'Did she hurt herself? Is she okay?' Whitney interrupted, her words tumbling out quicker than she'd intended. She clasped her hands together tightly, trying to steady them.

Lorraine nodded. 'She's fine physically. Only a few scratches. Luckily one of the team happened to be passing by her room and saw her lying on the floor and called for one of the others to assist. We got her up, but ever since then, she hasn't really known where she is. I'm sorry.'

Whitney's brow furrowed in worry, and she bit her lower lip. Her mum's confusion had been getting worse but she hadn't expected this.

'But she does drift in and out because of the dementia anyway,' said Whitney, trying to convince herself as much as Lorraine that it wasn't as bad as the manager was making it seem.

'Yes, but this time it's different. She appears to be in a permanent state of confusion.'

Whitney felt a cold shiver run down her spine. She looked down, avoiding Lorraine's gaze. 'Does she know her own name?'

Lorraine hesitated before answering, 'She didn't seem to.

We've called the doctor, and are waiting for someone to come out to visit her.'

'Shouldn't she go to the hospital?' Whitney's voice cracked slightly, revealing her underlying fear.

'We phoned 111 and explained the situation, and they felt a GP visit was more appropriate initially, rather than taking your mother to hospital because she doesn't seem hurt, just not herself. Also, the waiting times at A&E currently are horrendous. She's better off here in the comfort of her own home.'

Whitney nodded slowly, trying to process this information. She felt helpless, and her hands were clasped so tightly together that her knuckles had turned white.

'How do you know she's not hurt?'

'She was able to tell us when we asked her. She just didn't know who she was or where she was.'

Whitney's gaze drifted off, lost in thought. How much more of her mum would they lose? Her throat tightened at the thought.

'I need to see her,' Whitney said, standing. 'Is that okay?'

'Yes, of course. But remember, she's not doing well. So you'll need to brace yourself,' Lorraine said.

'Are you sure she's not going to get better?' Whitney asked, her heart aching at the thought of what she was about to see.

'I didn't say that,' Lorraine said softly. 'She may return to how she was before the fall, but I want you to prepare yourself in case she doesn't.'

'What does this mean in respect of her care here? Can she still stay, or will she have to go into a nursing home?'

'There'll be no change to her care at the moment. It's more her mental, rather than physical, requirements which have changed and we're perfectly capable of dealing with those.'

Whitney expelled the breath that she'd been holding. 'Thank goodness. Rob was meant to be visiting tomorrow. I don't want him to see her like this.'

'I understand. I've already been in touch with one of his carers, and we've decided to cancel the visit for now.'

'He'll be devastated. You know how much he looks forward to visiting. I'd take him out myself, except—' She paused for a moment.

'Is there an issue?'

Whitney sighed. 'We are in the middle of a murder investigation, and I know it shouldn't make any difference, but it might be difficult. I'll visit Rob after I've left here and explain the situation to him.'

'I think that's probably the best thing to do, for both of them. I'll come with you to see your mum. It might be distressing, but please don't show your feelings in front of her, because it could still upset her.'

'I understand,' Whitney said, fighting back the tears as they threatened to spill.

Lorraine slid over the box of tissues on her desk and Whitney took one, dabbing her eyes.

'I know it's upsetting and I'm sorry that I had to ask you in, but I didn't want to tell you on the phone about everything that had happened. Come on, let's go.'

They left the office and went upstairs to her mother's room. She was sitting on a chair beside the window. As they entered her room, the sun's rays streamed in, creating a warm ambience which was at odds with Whitney's mum, whose gaze was vague as she watched them.

'Hey, Mum,' Whitney said, running over her.

Her mother stared back at her, a blank expression on her face. 'Hello,' she said, her voice strange, stilted almost.

She doesn't recognise me. A lump formed in Whitney's throat.

'It's me, Mum. Your daughter, Whitney.'

'Hello... Whitney.'

'I came to see how you are. I understand you had a fall.'

'Yes, I fell,' her mum repeated.

'Have you hurt yourself?'

'No, I'm not hurt. Who are you?'

Whitney's heart sank. Tears formed in her eyes, which she fought back. Why didn't she remember?

'I'm Whitney. Your daughter. You remember me, don't you?' she repeated slowly, her voice cracking slightly.

'My daughter? Oh. I fell over.'

'Yes, I know. But you're okay, aren't you?'

'I think so.' She held out both arms in front of her and examined them.

Whitney turned and looked at Lorraine, her eyes brimming with tears, conveying a silent plea for understanding.

'Would you like a cup of tea, Mum? I can get you one,' Whitney asked, trying to sound hopeful.

'No, I don't drink tea.'

Whitney swallowed hard, the familiar sting of sadness intensifying. Mum loved her tea, so much. How could she forget that?

Lorraine shrugged and indicated with a tiny nod that they should leave.

'Okay, well, it was nice to see you, Mum. I'll come back and see you another time.'

She forced a smile, masking her growing despair.

'Yes, thank you. Goodbye. And what did you say your name is?'

'It's Whitney.' Whitney's voice was barely above a whisper, her smile faltering.

'Goodbye, Whitney.'

As Whitney walked away, her shoulders slumped, a wave of grief and loss washing over her. Her heart was heavy with the harsh realities of her mother's dementia. *It's like I'm losing her piece by piece.*

Lorraine guided Whitney out of the room, and as they

headed down the corridor, Whitney turned to the manager. 'This is awful. But you're hopeful that she's going to get better. That's what you said, isn't it?'

'I hope she will, but be prepared in case she doesn't. Hopefully it's the shock of the fall that's made her disorientated, and she'll gradually come right and—'

'How can you be sure?' Whitney interrupted. 'She could stay like that from now on.'

'In my experience, she will get a bit better. Maybe not back to how she was, but there will be an improvement.'

'Will she recognise me again?' Whitney held her breath, praying that the woman would say yes.

'We hope so. Try not to worry... Yes, I know that's a silly thing to say, but know that she's in the best place. We're taking very good care of her.'

'When shall I come and see her again?' Whitney asked, sucking in a breath.

'I'll get in touch with you once the doctor's been and we've got a better idea of your mum's prognosis. Are you going to see Rob now, to make sure he's okay about not visiting tomorrow?'

'Yes, that's my next stop.'

Whitney left the home and sat in her car, tears streaming down her face. She couldn't let Rob see her like that, so she sat there for a while until she could pull herself together. Tiffany was going to be devastated. She loved her grandma.

Whitney drove to the assisted-living facility where Rob lived, a large, modern detached house.

After knocking, the door was answered by Gwen. 'Hi, I've come to see Rob.'

'Is he expecting you?'

'No, it's a surprise visit. But before I go in, you need to know that our mum has had a fall.'

'We've already been told. That's why his visit was cancelled.'

'The situation isn't good. The fall seems to have affected her memory. She had no idea who I was. I'm hoping it might be temporary, but bearing in mind how she was already going downhill, we have no idea what's going to happen. I wanted to let Rob know. When I leave, he may be upset.'

'I'm so sorry to hear about her. Thanks for letting me know. Rob's in the lounge watching telly with a couple of the other residents.'

'Thanks,' Whitney said as she walked down to the TV room. Standing at the door, she looked at her brother. He was a great big man, but really a child trapped in a man's body. After many years, they'd recently discovered who had attacked him and brought the person to justice. It had helped Rob regain some memory of that time, but other than that, it didn't change him.

'Rob,' she called out quietly.

He turned around. 'Whitney,' he exclaimed, jumping up from his seat and enveloping her in a big bear hug. 'You didn't say you were coming today.'

'I know, it's a surprise visit. Let's go to your room. I want to talk to you about something.'

'But I'm watching the telly. It's my programme.'

'I won't take long, because I've got some work to do.'

'You do have a very important job,' he said, nodding. 'I understand.'

They went to his room, and she sat on the chair whilst he perched on the edge of the bed. 'I've got something serious to tell you. It's Mum.'

'Yes, I know she fell over and hurt herself, and that's why I can't go to see her tomorrow. I've made a cake for us. Would you like some of my cake? It's chocolate. I know that's Mum's favourite.'

'Not just now. But I do want to say more about the fall. Mum's okay – she didn't break any of her bones.'

'That's good, because she wouldn't want to have her arm in plaster like I once had.'

'No, she wouldn't want that,' Whitney said. 'But it seems to have affected her memory. She doesn't remember everything.'

'Yes, I know. You told me that before. That's something to do with what she's got. Her densha.'

'It's sort of to do with her *dementia*, yes,' Whitney said, emphasising the pronunciation. 'It's made her dementia a little bit worse now, and she's not sure at the moment who everybody is.'

'She'll know me,' he said.

'Well, yes, I'm sure she will. But, when I went to see her, she had forgotten my name.'

'Oh, and you think she's not going to remember me?'

'We don't know yet. We're waiting for the doctor to visit to see what they can do for her.' Whitney's voice was soft, trying to sound reassuring despite her own uncertainties.

'Will they give her some medicine to make her remember things?'

Whitney sighed, looking down briefly. *If only it were that simple.*

'I think they might give her something, but for the time being it's best that you don't visit. I don't want you to get upset about it. And you mustn't think that Mum doesn't love you, because she does.'

'I know she loves me. She loves me lots. I'm her best boy. She always says that.'

'Because you are. And you're my best boy as well.'

'Is Tiffany with you? I want to see Ava.'

'Not at the moment. But we're going to sort out a time for us all to go out together. You, me, Tiffany, and Ava.'

'And Mum.'

'We don't know whether Mum will be able to come. But if

she can, we definitely will go together, because we're one big family, aren't we?' Whitney's voice wavered slightly.

'That's right, we are.'

'So, I'm very sorry about tomorrow, but I'll be in touch, and I'll let you know how Mum is.' As she finished speaking, Whitney gave a small, somewhat forced smile, her heart heavy.

'Can I go back to watch my programme now? I might have some cake. Would you like some, Whitney?'

'I'm not hungry at the moment. Why don't I take some home for me to have later with Tiffany and Ava?'

'Oh yes, that's a good idea,' he said excitedly, jumping up. 'Let's go to the kitchen, and I'll wrap a piece up for you.'

She followed him into the kitchen, and he pulled out a cake tin and opened it. 'Look, isn't it lovely?'

She stared at the round cake covered in streaky chocolate icing with hundreds and thousands sprinkled on top. 'Yum... It certainly looks delicious. Where are the knives?'

'I'm not allowed to touch them without anyone being with me. I'll get someone to come in.'

He disappeared, leaving her in the room, and she peered again at the cake. He'd done a very good job of the icing. In another world, he could well have been a chef.

Rob returned with Gwen. 'I'm giving Whitney some cake because Mum couldn't have any, and I need to cut her some slices.'

'Okay,' Gwen said, taking a key out of her pocket and opening a cupboard that was kept padlocked. She took out a knife. 'There you go, you can cut whilst I'm here watching.'

Rob methodically cut three equal pieces, took some cling film and wrapped them. He then gave them to Whitney.

'Thanks, Rob. We'll really enjoy the cake later,' Whitney said.

Her brother handed the knife to the carer, who washed it up and replaced it in the cupboard.

'I'm going back to watch telly now. Is that okay, Whitney?'

'Of course, you big lump,' she said affectionately, giving him a cuddle. He returned the hug and then ran out of the room in the direction of the TV room.

'He seems fine,' she said to Gwen. 'I've explained about Mum. Not sure that he properly understood the implications, but I'll arrange to visit him with Tiffany and Ava. I'm not exactly sure when. We're in the middle of a difficult case. I'll keep you informed if there's any more news on Mum's condition.'

SEVENTEEN

Thursday

Whitney's grip on her mug of triple-strength coffee tightened slightly as she stepped into the incident room. Her eyes scanned the familiar faces of her team, each absorbed in their tasks. The clatter of keyboards and murmur of low conversations filled the space. She'd been working since six-thirty that morning, hoping that it would take her mind off her family problems. But it hadn't worked, and she'd struggled to focus.

As she approached the whiteboard, she set her mug down on the table with a soft thud, the sound seeming louder in her own ears.

'You all right, guv?' Frank's voice broke through her thoughts, pulling her back to the present.

Whitney glanced over at him, her frown deepening. 'Why do you ask?' she replied, unable to hide the weariness in her voice.

'Because you look dreadful – like you've either had a night out on the tiles or you haven't been able to sleep.' Frank's brows were knitted in concern as he scrutinised her.

Whitney attempted a reassuring smile. 'No, it's fine. I've got a few issues with my mum, that's all.' Her voice was firmer now, an attempt to brush off the concern.

'Is she okay?' Frank's worry was evident as he slightly leant forwards in his anxiousness for her response.

Whitney sighed internally, appreciating his concern but not wanting to delve too deeply into her personal matters. Not that she wanted to hide it from them. That wasn't how the team worked. They had always shared their lives with each other; a bond forged through countless hours spent together in this very room.

'I hope so. Anyway, we can't discuss this now.' She redirected the focus to work, finding solace in the familiarity of their routine. 'Let's get started. I've no idea what time Dr Cavendish will be arriving, but we can't wait. When—'

She was interrupted by the door opening and George striding into the room.

'We were talking about you,' Frank said with a chuckle, lightening the mood.

George's expression shifted to one of confusion. She looked directly at Whitney. 'Am I late? Is there a problem?'

'No, you're not late at all. We didn't know when you'd be coming in. It's fine,' Whitney explained, offering a small nod. She hoped George could read the unspoken message in her eyes – that there was more to discuss about her mum, but not here, not now.

'Please continue,' George said, heading towards Whitney and standing close by.

Whitney turned back to the task at hand, feeling the weight of leadership heavy on her shoulders. 'Okay, let's talk about what we've got already. We now know, because we found a notebook in Valerie Jenkins' room, that, along with Angus McDonnell, she was planning to discredit Hargrove's theory.

We need to find out exactly how they were going to do that. Also what connects McDonnell and Jenkins?' The answers they needed were somewhere in the room – in the notebooks, on the laptops, within the team – and she was determined to find them. 'Ellie, I'd like you to work on that. Make that a priority,' Whitney directed, trying to mask the undercurrent of fatigue in her voice.

'Yes, guv,' Ellie responded, with a quick nod. 'But you know I've already been working on it, because you asked me to start yesterday. Remember?'

Whitney glanced at Ellie, noticing the shadows under her eyes, a mirror to her own restless night. She made a mental note to suggest the officer take a break after the case was resolved.

'Of course. Sorry. I forgot.' Whitney rubbed her temple as if to physically stimulate her memory. 'So, what have you found out about McDonnell and Jenkins?'

'First of all, they are connected. McDonnell and Jenkins were due to present at a conference in Brussels later in the year, but they withdrew,' Ellie informed everyone.

'Oh, I know that conference,' George said. 'It's most prestigious. I was planning on attending. Do you know what they were going to present?'

'According to the abstract in the conference agenda, something about a new theory relating to serial killers that could change current thinking.'

Whitney's brow furrowed. 'Did that mean they'd intended on ripping off Hargrove's theory?'

'I would suspect not *ripping off*, but possibly they're working together so they could discredit Hargrove's theory and replace it with their own as an alternative. If they didn't take that approach, it's possible that no one would be interested in their theory,' George speculated, her expression serious and contemplative.

'It doesn't seem a very good way of working to me. But you're the expert on that,' Whitney commented. Academia wasn't her world, and the politics of it often seemed unnecessarily convoluted.

'That's higher education for you,' George replied with a sigh, shrugging slightly as if to emphasise her resignation of what happened in her workplace. 'Academic reputations are often gained and lost at the expense of other people's theories. It's extremely cut-throat. Some people think if you work in higher education, you're on a different level to others because of your intellect, but at times it can be extremely petty and quite nasty.'

'Yes, I remember you mentioning this to me in the past,' Whitney said, her nod slow and thoughtful. It was a world so different from her own, where facts and evidence led the way, as opposed to the whims of academic prestige. 'But why drop out of the conference?'

'That is puzzling,' George answered. 'That particular conference is usually oversubscribed with submissions and to withdraw after publication of the programme could go against them in the future. Except... now Jenkins is dead, it puts a different complexion on it.'

'But they dropped out before she died. Why? Knowing might help the investigation, don't you think?' Whitney asked, looking directly at George for confirmation.

'Possibly,' George agreed.

'Okay, so Jenkins and Hargrove— I mean, Jenkins and McDonnell were working together to discredit Hargrove's theory, and now Hargrove's dead. Could they have killed him because they were unsuccessful? With Hargrove out the way, they can put forward their view without anyone to challenge them. But then why kill Jenkins?' Whitney mused aloud, her gaze drifting to the whiteboard, as if the answers might be written there.

'What about if McDonnell decided he wanted to take all the credit and so got rid of them both, guv?' Frank suggested, looking pleased with himself.

'That's certainly an option,' Whitney agreed. 'George?'

'We have no evidence of that. Ellie, was there anywhere else the pair had been offered to present their theory?' George asked, leaning against the edge of a desk. 'There are many conferences across Europe where they could have applied.'

'That's the only one I could find,' Ellie said, glancing up. 'But I'll keep checking.'

'It's possible they had a disagreement and that's why they withdrew,' George speculated.

'We don't have any proof relating to a falling-out, though,' Whitney said. 'Certainly not in her notebook.'

'That is a good point. One would have thought something would have been mentioned.'

'Let's park that for now. What have we found relating to Hargrove?' Whitney asked the rest of the team, redirecting the conversation. 'Do we know whether Hargrove knew about Jenkins and McDonnell's theory and their intent to discredit him?'

Ellie, scrolling through her notes, seemed focused but drained. 'I did find something on an academic forum. Hargrove was openly challenging anyone to refute his theory, and to provide evidence.'

Whitney raised an eyebrow. 'And did he actually name Jenkins and McDonnell in his posts?'

'No, but it was in response to a criticism that McDonnell had made about the theory on the forum,' Ellie replied, her fingers pausing on the keyboard as she looked up. 'Hargrove said no one could challenge him because they lacked his credibility.'

Whitney turned to George, seeking her insight. 'Is that right, George? Did Hargrove have the credibility he claimed?'

George leant against the wall, arms crossed, a thoughtful expression on her face. 'He was certainly credible in his field. But his theories were too extreme for many traditional theorists.'

Whitney sighed, feeling the weight of the case. 'Okay, so we know there's antagonism between Hargrove, Jenkins, and McDonnell. But now Jenkins is dead. How does that relate?'

'We have Hargrove going up to his room after the morning sessions on Monday,' Frank said. 'Before his death.'

Whitney nodded, her mind racing with possibilities. 'Right, and McDonnell? Was he anywhere close by?'

'He did use the stairs around that time,' Frank said, shifting uncomfortably, 'But I was unable to see where he came out because the cameras are focused on the lifts.'

Whitney's frustration grew, and she rubbed her temples, feeling the onset of a headache. 'So, he went up the stairs, but we don't know where. We know he wasn't staying there, so what was he doing? What time did he come down?'

'I don't know,' Frank said, shrugging helplessly.

Whitney let out a deep breath. 'Great, that doesn't really help us much, does it? Right, what about the people who attended Hargrove's Sunday session?'

'All academics are legitimately there,' Meena said.

Whitney paced a little, her mind racing. 'Okay, right. We need to bring in Angus McDonnell for questioning. He's the link between Jenkins and Hargrove. We need to find out exactly how the three of them are connected.'

'Also, we shouldn't forget that McDonnell himself might be in danger,' Doug said. 'Maybe the three of them are being targeted?'

'Yes, that had crossed my mind, and that's another reason for interviewing the man. Brian, instruct uniform to go to the conference centre and bring him in. Assuming he's there. If he isn't, they can try the university.'

As she spoke, Whitney couldn't help but feel a pang of guilt about her mother and brother. She was here, trying to solve a case, whilst her family needed her. But duty called, and she knew she had to focus. Her team depended on her, and she couldn't let her personal life interfere with her professional responsibilities. Still, the concern for her family lingered in the back of her mind, a constant, nagging presence.

EIGHTEEN

Thursday

'What are you going to do?' George asked Whitney after her friend had explained about the issue with her mother.

They were sitting in the station's café, taking a much-needed quick break whilst waiting for Angus McDonnell to be brought in.

'I'm caught between a rock and a hard place, as the saying goes,' Whitney replied. 'What can I do? It's impossible for her to live with me. All I can do is hope that she gets some of her memory back and she remembers us, because Rob will be devastated if she doesn't. Tiffany, too. After I told Rob last night, I could see he was upset, even though I'm not sure that he totally understood. It really is a question of wait and see. When you think back to what Mum was like it's heartbreaking. Do you remember when you met her? She was a bit forgetful, but nothing like this. You seriously wouldn't recognise her now.' Whitney gave a resigned shrug. 'Anyway, tell me how the wedding preparations are going.'

George took a sip of her coffee. 'The same as it is every time you ask. We're getting there, slowly. I'll be relieved when it's all over.'

'At least you're not turning into a bridezilla, thank goodness. I couldn't have coped. It would've been the last straw.'

'A bridezilla?' George repeated, having no idea to what Whitney was referring.

'You know, one of those...' Whitney gesticulated with her arms.

'I'm afraid I don't.'

'It's a comparison with Godzilla, you know the giant lizard that rampages through the city in the films? Anyway, it means a crazy, totally irrational, bonkers bride. You must have seen them on the telly.'

'No, I haven't. And I'm not crazy, obviously. Why would I be?' George asked, frowning.

She wasn't into popular culture like her friend. Never had been, and she suspected never would be. She much preferred reading a good book to watching endless TV.

'Well, good. I'm glad you're not. Are you looking forward to the wedding yet?'

George gave a small shrug. 'I'll be glad when it's all over. I'm happy for Ross to have his family present, but... I'm not... not looking forward to it,' George said, reluctant to admit her true feelings even to Whitney.

'You do make me laugh. Even if you're acting all nonplussed about it, I'm looking forward to the big day. It's going to be great and you're going to look beautiful. It will be a day to remember.'

'If you say so.' She would much rather be the centre of attention when giving a lecture in front of two hundred students, and not walking down the aisle in front of everyone she knew.

Whitney's phone rang, and she picked it up. 'Hello.' She paused, nodding. 'Okay, we'll be there shortly.' She ended the call and turned to George. 'McDonnell's arrived. We'll collect

Brian and get the ear mics. I'll take this with me; there's still some left,' she said, picking up her coffee.

'That's a good idea. It will help you focus and keep you from being so distracted.'

Whitney's coffee addiction was a well-known fact.

'You're not wrong there,' Whitney laughed.

When they reached the interview room, George went into the observation area and stared at McDonnell, who was sitting alone. He appeared twitchy, but not necessarily guilty.

'Good morning, Dr McDonnell. Thanks for coming in,' Whitney said when she entered the room with Brian and they took seats opposite him.

'I didn't have a choice. I was brought in, and I'm not sure why. It—'

'If you could wait one moment,' Whitney said, holding up a hand to silence him. 'Brian, start the recording, please.'

'Interview on Thursday, fourteenth of March. Those present: DCI Walker, DS Chapman, and... please state your name for the recording,' Brian said.

'Dr Angus McDonnell.'

'Dr McDonnell, we have several questions that we'd like to ask you regarding the deaths of Jonathan Hargrove and Valerie Jenkins,' Whitney said.

McDonnell tensed, his eyes wide. His shock appeared genuine, but he could be acting.

'Valerie's dead?' he uttered, his voice breaking slightly.

'You haven't heard? Weren't you at the conference yesterday?' Whitney asked.

'I didn't go in the end. I was too busy with work, and I haven't been this morning either. Nobody told me. I haven't spoken to anybody,' he said, the words tumbling quickly from his mouth.

Too quickly?

George needed to witness further reactions.

'Pursue this, Whitney,' George requested. 'I wish to assess his responses. The speed of his speech has increased and his pitch is slightly higher than earlier.'

Whitney gave a tiny nod, confirming she was going to do as asked.

'Why didn't you go yesterday?' Whitney asked, leaning forwards slightly.

McDonnell sat upright in his chair, his hands clasped together nervously in his lap. 'I told you, I had work to do. Marking.'

'So it was nothing to do with the fact that Hargrove was now dead and you didn't feel the need to be there?' Whitney prodded, sharply.

He shifted uncomfortably, avoiding eye contact. 'Well, the reason I'd gone in the first place was obviously to see him, to make a point of challenging his theory.'

'And then, of course, he wasn't there, so you didn't bother to go again?' Whitney said sceptically.

'Well, like I said, I'm busy,' McDonnell said, defensively while fidgeting.

'We have discovered messages on Jonathan Hargrove's phone between the two of you. You want to discredit his theory, so he threatened you with divulging something that happened years ago.' Whitney's statement was like a trap snapping shut.

McDonnell coloured slightly, his facial expression betraying his guilt. 'Yes.'

'What was he going to reveal?' Whitney pressed on.

'It's nothing. Well, it's not nothing, but it happened years ago at university.' He glanced away, his voice barely above a whisper.

'If it happened years ago, why does it matter?'

'Because in our world, everything matters.' His voice was a mix of fear and frustration.

'He's correct about that,' George said.

'You need to tell us more,' Whitney insisted.

McDonnell looked up, his eyes filled with a plea for discretion. 'If I do... is it confidential? I want your assurance that it won't go any further, because it could end my career.'

'I can't make any assurances, but I think there are more serious matters to worry about. You're a suspect in the murder of Jonathan Hargrove. We need to know everything.'

'I didn't kill him, I promise. I didn't kill him.'

'So, why were there these messages between the two of you? And if he could discredit you and ruin your whole career, surely that's motive enough? Why don't you tell us what it is?'

'I was awarded the Hamilton Medal for academic excellence.'

'Yes, we know about that. It's a very prestigious award and must've gone a long way in helping your career,' Whitney said, leaning forward, sounding intrigued.

'Yes, it was.' McDonnell stared directly ahead, his fingers drumming on the table, lips pressed tightly together. His body was rigid, typical of someone struggling to decide whether or not to unburden himself.

'The medal is at the heart of this, Whitney. Keep pursuing it.' George's voice was low, almost a whisper, as if sharing a confidential secret.

'Dr McDonnell, I can see that there's something you're not telling me about this medal. I suggest that changes. Now.' Whitney's tone was firm and uncompromising.

'Okay.' He let out a long sigh. 'The medal was awarded for my work using Jungian analytical psychology to interpret the motives and actions of criminals. But my findings were fabricated, and Jonathan found out.'

George sucked in a breath. 'This is huge.'

'Wow. That's bad on so many levels, isn't it?' Whitney said, unable to hide her disbelief at his actions.

'Yes,' McDonnell muttered, his gaze dropping to his hands, which were now clasped together tightly.

'How did Hargrove find out?' Whitney prodded, anxious for the whole story.

'I accidentally left some work in the library. He picked it up to return it to me. In those days, we weren't doing so much online. Most of it was handwritten, and although we did type things up, I had pages of notes. He found my book, he brought it to me, having read it, and he accused me of being a cheat.'

'Did he threaten to expose you?'

'No. We were students at the time, in our twenties. What he said was that I would owe him one day.'

'And he didn't mention it to anyone?' Whitney asked.

'No. I got the medal, and we left university and went our separate ways. He did better than me, anyway.' McDonnell's voice held a note of resignation, his gaze drifting off, as if lost in the past.

'When did he bring it up?'

'When he found out that Valerie and I were working on a theory that was similar to his, but with modifications, because we believed that he hadn't considered certain aspects.'

'I see. So, you and Valerie wanted to discredit his theory and then take the limelight for this new approach to serial killers.'

'Yes.'

'And you're saying that Jonathan Hargrove used his knowledge about what you'd done in the past to try and stop you from doing that?'

'Yes, that's exactly what he did,' McDonnell replied in earnest.

'Okay, so really, you wanted Hargrove out of the way because of his threats?'

'I thought we might come to some arrangement. But we didn't get that far because he died.'

'Which, of course, you know nothing about,' Whitney said, challenging McDonnell to contradict her.

'I've already explained about that when you came to see me with Dr Cavendish.'

'As well as arguing with Professor Hargrove outside the restaurant on Monday morning, you also took the stairs in the accommodation area at a time when he'd gone to his room.'

'That's right, I went up to see Jonathan,' McDonnell admitted, his voice steady but his hands fidgeting, betraying a hint of nervousness.

'How did you know he was there?'

'He left the conference and I assumed he'd gone to his room,' McDonnell responded, avoiding direct eye contact.

'So you must have been one of the last people to see him alive.'

'I don't know, I suppose so.' McDonnell's words were accompanied by a shrug, an attempt at nonchalance that didn't quite mask the underlying tension.

'What happened?'

'I went to his room and knocked on the door. When he answered, I said we needed to speak, but he said not now because he was expecting someone else.' McDonnell's brow furrowed as he recalled the moment.

'What?' Whitney snapped. 'Why didn't you tell us this before? Surely you realised that it was important for our investigation.'

'I didn't want to be involved in case you thought I had something to do with it.' McDonnell's voice rose slightly in pitch, a sign of his growing anxiety. 'I went to see him, it was a one-minute chat, if that, and then I left the conference.'

'Why did you take the stairs and not the lift?'

'I hate lifts.' McDonnell replied a bit too quickly.

'And did anyone see you?'

'No,' McDonnell whispered.

'So you have no alibi.'

'I didn't kill Jonathan Hargrove, and I know he had dirt on me, but that's not who I am,' McDonnell asserted, his voice trembling.

'Well, it's looking very different from our perspective,' Whitney said. She paused before continuing, as if letting the words percolate through McDonnell's mind. 'Let's talk about Valerie Jenkins now. I understand that you were working together on an alternative theory, and that you'd arranged to present it in Brussels, but then dropped out. Is that correct?'

'Yes.' McDonnell's reply was brief, his voice tight. 'How do you know?'

'Because I have researchers and it's their job to find out. The conference in Brussels is extremely prestigious so your reason for pulling out must have been good. Was it because you were no longer working with Valerie Jenkins?'

'It's complicated.' McDonnell sighed, looking down momentarily before returning to look at Whitney again.

'Well, uncomplicate it,' Whitney said, unyielding.

'Valerie and I had a relationship,' he admitted, his voice dropping.

'He's married,' George interjected, and Whitney nodded in acknowledgement.

'Okay. Are you referring to a sexual relationship?'

'Yes,' McDonnell replied, his face flushing slightly.

'I understand you're married. So, you had an affair with Valerie?'

'We did, but I ended it because my wife was getting suspicious.' McDonnell's voice was filled with regret, his hands clasped together.

'Okay. So your affair coming to an end meant you couldn't continue working together on this theory?'

'I wanted us to carry on working as colleagues, but Valerie refused.'

'Were you surprised by that?'

'Yes because she was obsessed with discrediting Hargrove... until I found out the real reason.'

'Which was?' Whitney asked.

'She wanted our affair to continue and told me we could only work together under those circumstances.'

'How did you respond to this?'

'Initially I refused, then she threatened to send my wife photos of us together and—'

There was a knock, and Ellie poked her head around the door, interrupting the tense atmosphere.

'Guv, I've got something I need to tell you.'

'Okay. Interview suspended.'

Whitney and Brian headed out into the corridor and George left the observation area to meet them.

'I've discovered that Angus McDonnell's wife is diabetic, so he would have access to insulin,' Ellie said.

'That's excellent work. Well done. Unless anyone has an issue, I'll charge him.' Whitney's voice was resolute.

'Fine by me, guv,' Brian said.

'I agree,' George added. 'He has a strong motivation for seeing both of them dead.'

George returned to observing and watched as Whitney and Brian entered the room.

'Angus McDonnell, I'm arresting you on suspicion of the murders of Jonathan Hargrove and Valerie Jenkins. You do not have to say anything, but it may harm your defence if you do not mention something which you later rely on in court. Anything you do say may be given in evidence. Do you understand?' Whitney said.

'What? What are you talking about? I need my solicitor.'

McDonnell's voice was panicked, his face a mix of shock and fear.

'You will be escorted to the custody suite, and you can phone your solicitor from there.'

NINETEEN

Friday

Whitney walked jauntily into the station, unable to hide the lift in her spirits, compared with the previous day. Lorraine from her mum's care home had called a few minutes before Whitney left the house that morning to let her know there'd been a marked improvement in her mum's condition and that she was slowly becoming her old self. She knew where she was and had recognised some of the carers. The news had been a massive relief.

She went into her office, hung up her jacket on the peg, placed her handbag on the back of her chair and made her way to the incident room. The whole team had already arrived. It wasn't that she was late, but clearly the urgency of the murders had driven everyone to start their day early.

'Good morning, everybody,' Whitney greeted, her voice filled with the cheer she felt. She placed her coffee on the table near the whiteboard, a subconscious anchor in the room's dynamic.

'You're sounding a lot better, guv,' Frank said, passing comment, as usual. 'Is everything okay with your mum?'

Whitney glanced at the officer, appreciating his concern. 'Thank you, Frank, yes, I am. She's improving. Add that to the fact that we've got Angus McDonnell in custody and it's already starting to look like a good day. We're waiting for his solicitor to arrive, yes?'

'He can't be a very important client if his solicitor couldn't make it yesterday,' Doug said, leaning back in his chair with his arms folded.

Whitney shot Doug a small, knowing smile. 'I believe the solicitor was on annual leave yesterday, and McDonnell particularly wanted to wait for him. It's fine by me because it's given us more time to get all our Ts crossed and our Is dotted.'

Brian, who had been shuffling papers at his desk, looked up with concern. 'What about Dr Cavendish? Is she coming in today? Don't we need her input?'

'She's attending the conference,' Whitney replied, her eyes scanning the room, noting the team's reactions.

'It's a bloody long conference,' Frank said, a grimace on his face.

Whitney nodded in agreement, a slight smile playing on her lips. 'Yes, it certainly seems so. Between you and me, it sounds deathly boring. I've never been to a conference that's lasted longer than three days and even then there's usually only one or two sessions I really enjoy. It's clearly different in the academic world.'

'Actually, most of them aren't that long,' Ellie, who had been quietly typing at her computer, added.

Whitney glanced at the officer, noticing that she was still peaky, but there had been an improvement. 'So now we all know. Anyway, back to today, I want everything in place in time for the interview. I believe the solicitor's due to arrive at ten-thirty, which gives us an hour and a bit.' She paused, taking a moment to gather her thoughts. 'Let's continue researching into McDonnell, Jenkins, and Hargrove. We need to make sure we've got all those links tied up. Have there been any financial links between the three of them?'

'We couldn't find anything, guv,' Brian said.

'Thanks. It was worth investigating.'

As Whitney spoke, the burden of responsibility weighed heavily on her shoulders. She knew the team looked to her for guidance, and she couldn't let her personal issues interfere with the investigation. But as she sipped her coffee, her mind briefly wandered back to her mum and brother, and their situations, grateful that things seemed to be returning to how they were.

Whitney's phone vibrated in her pocket. She pulled it out, her brow furrowing as she saw George's name flash across the screen. 'Morning, George, how are you?' she answered.

'Sorry, Whitney, I have some bad news,' George said, her voice urgent. 'Hargrove's research assistant, Dr Toby Merchant, has been found dead.'

Whitney's heart skipped a beat. 'What?' she exclaimed, her voice rising in disbelief. She glanced quickly at her team, noticing their concerned expressions. She subtly shook her head, indicating that something was wrong but not divulging the details yet.

'Tell me what happened.' She gripped the phone tighter, bracing herself for more unsettling news.

'He was found in the summer house of the conference centre's grounds.'

'By whom?' she asked, her mind racing, trying to piece together the emerging situation.

'One of the gardeners, and it was purely by chance,' George replied.

Whitney's thoughts whirled. Another death at the conference? Her concern deepened. It was spiralling out of control.

'How do you know all this?' she enquired, her detective instincts kicking in.

'I arrived early intending to speak to another psychologist regarding a conference we're attending next year and I noticed a police car arrive. I walked outside and went to investigate,' George explained.

Whitney nodded slowly, even though George couldn't see her. She appreciated her friend's diligence.

'What did you tell them?'

'I informed them there had been two other deaths at the conference, and they told me about this one. I believe the pathologist has been called,' George continued.

'How come this is the first I've heard of it?' she asked, frustrated at the oversight.

'Because it's only just happened. I think uniformed officers called it in,' George replied.

Whitney's mind raced with the implications of this new development. 'We need to bring the conference to a close, or at least ensure everyone is kept there. Yes... that's better. We'll keep them all in the one place. Where are the delegates now?' Whitney's voice was firm, and she tapped her fingers impatiently on the desk she was leaning against.

'The keynote lecture is due to start shortly, so everyone should be there.'

Whitney nodded thoughtfully, as she visualised the conference layout. 'We'll need to interview everyone. I want you to take charge in my absence. Make sure nobody leaves.' Her words were decisive, leaving no room for doubt. The weight of responsibility on her shoulders just became heavier.

'No problem,' George said. 'I'll liaise with conference organisers and centre management.'

'If anyone queries you, explain that you're acting on behalf of the police. Keep everyone in one space, if possible. I'm assuming the main conference area is best. And you think the pathologist has been called?' Whitney asked to double check.

'Yes.'

'We need to make sure that it's Claire. Leave that with me. I'll be with you shortly. Great work, by the way.'

'Thank you,' George replied. 'I'll wait for you in reception.'

Whitney ended the call, her heart pounding with a mix of dread and determination. She looked to her team, attempting to keep her expression serious but composed. 'You may or may not have guessed what that's all about, but in case you didn't... We have another dead body.'

'Well, they can't have been murdered by McDonnell then. He was in custody all night,' Frank called out, his eyes wide with shock.

'Exactly, and he can stay there for now. We don't know if the deaths are linked, or even if the latest is suspicious. It's the research assistant to Jonathan Hargrove, Dr Toby Merchant,' Whitney explained.

'Bloody hell, it seems to always happen that we have a suspect in custody only for someone else to be murdered. It's like some sort of sick joke,' Frank said, waving his arms around.

'Don't exaggerate, Frank. Occasionally we might arrest the wrong person, but that's all part of the investigation process. Ellie, you need to do your magic on Toby Merchant. Find everything you can on him,' Whitney instructed. 'Frank and Doug, I want you to check CCTV to see where Merchant has been over the past few days.' Her hands were clasped in front of her in a gesture of focused determination.

'Yes, guv,' the officers said in unison.

'Meena and Brian, look at social media accounts belonging to each of our victims. See if we can do some linking. Obviously, Merchant and Hargrove will link because they work together, but aside from that,' she added, her mind already formulating the next steps of their investigation. 'And Brian, please phone pathology to ensure it's Claire who's been sent out. You know where I am if you need me.'

TWENTY

Friday

George stood at the entrance to the conference centre, her foot rhythmically tapping on the ground. An air of impatience enveloped her as she craned her neck, scanning for Whitney's arrival. She'd already briefed the conference organisers, instructing them to ensure everyone was kept in the main area. George's mind raced with the potential reactions of the academics confined inside – undoubtedly, they would be itching with curiosity about the unfolding drama.

Finally, two vehicles approached – Whitney's familiar, well-worn Ford Focus, trailing behind Claire's MGC, a car George had long admired. The sight of them brought a slight relief. She quick-stepped over to Whitney as she parked.

'Is everything okay?' Whitney's voice cut through George's thoughts.

With a nod, George confirmed the situation. 'The conference organisers are ensuring everyone is kept in the main conference room. I thought it best to come out here and wait for you. I assume you wish to view the body?'

Their conversation was briefly interrupted as Claire joined them.

'Morning, Claire. Good to see you again,' Whitney said.

'If you say so. Now, where's this body?' Claire demanded.

'In the summer house,' George responded, pointing in front of them and slightly to the left. 'Take the path around the side of the building and you'll come across the area where there's a police cordon set up.'

'We'll follow you down there, as we haven't been to the scene yet because I've only just arrived,' Whitney said. 'And before you say anything, yes we'll keep out of your way.'

'Thank you. That's much appreciated,' the pathologist responded as she marched off in the direction of the summer house.

Whitney's mouth dropped open. 'Am I dreaming? Did Claire just offer her thanks?'

'Yes, she did.'

'Bloody hell, wonders will never cease. I wonder what's got into her.' She shook her head. 'Did you notice the bright orange trousers tucked into knee-high tan suede boots with tassels. Combining them with the pale-pink-and-mint-green checked jacket was an interesting choice, to say the least. Don't you agree?'

'I can't say I paid any attention,' George responded.

'I don't believe you.'

George shook her head slightly, her eyes briefly following Claire's colourful figure as she headed away from them. 'Whitney, you're not going to draw me into a discussion on Claire's wardrobe. We had this conversation only a few days ago.'

'Yes, I know,' Whitney conceded, a slight chuckle escaping her lips despite appearing to try to suppress it. 'But I don't get why you don't find it as funny as I do.'

George's expression didn't change. 'There's no need for meanness.'

'I'm not doing it in a mean way. Claire has her own style, but I'm allowed to point it out occasionally,' Whitney said.

'Except it's more than occasional. As you mentioned, it's Claire's style. We've known her for many years and I'm surprised that recently you've felt the need to comment so often,' George added, her stance firm, unyielding to Whitney's light-hearted banter.

'All right, all right,' Whitney said, holding up a hand in a mock surrender, her face breaking into a grin. 'I'm sorry. I'll try not to in the future, but I do think today's outfit is one of the good ones.'

'Right, let's go down there,' George said, redirecting their focus to the task at hand.

They walked behind Claire, maintaining a professional distance until reaching the cordoned-off summer house. They ducked under the cordon, having signed in with the police officer on duty and then walked closer to the summer house and stood at the entrance.

'He's seated. How come he didn't fall over?' Whitney asked, looking at Merchant's body, her brows knitting in confusion.

'I'm not sure,' George replied, as she studied the body, her eyes tracing the outline of the seated figure, searching for clues in its positioning.

'Claire,' Whitney called out, her voice echoing slightly in the open space.

'Yes?'

'Was he moved post-mortem into that position?'

'Whitney, I'm not prepared to start coming up with guesses,' Claire responded sternly, her focus on the body unwavering.

George observed silently, crossing her arms as she took in the scene, trying to piece together the possible scenarios in her mind.

'I was wondering why he hadn't fallen to the side,' Whitney

said loud enough for Claire to hear, but the pathologist didn't respond.

'Perhaps his weight is so evenly distributed, only his head flopped forwards slightly when he died,' George suggested, peering intently at the scene, seeking answers.

'Good point. There also doesn't appear to be a visible cause of death. Claire, can we assume it's insulin poisoning?' Whitney asked.

'When the body's at the morgue, I'll know better,' Claire replied with a frustrated sigh, her hands on her hips as she stared down at the body.

'Okay, I get it. It's fine,' Whitney conceded, her shoulders slumping slightly in resignation. 'But I'll be assuming that's what it is until you tell me otherwise. Any idea of time of death?'

'Judging by the body temperature, I can give you an approximate time of death of between ten p.m. and four a.m.,' Claire finally offered.

Whitney glanced at George, her eyebrows raised in silent communication. George nodded slightly, acknowledging the information and its implications. That was very generous of the pathologist, considering her usual responses.

'Thanks, Claire. Let's go,' Whitney said to George, turning to leave the scene.

George's stride was steady and controlled, her mind already racing ahead to the next steps of their investigation. An expression of deep concentration was on Whitney's face, a mirror to George's own thoughts as the complexities of the case continued to unravel.

When they were out of earshot, Whitney turned to George. 'Well, at least we've been given some sort of time frame from Claire. That's something, I suppose. Now we'll have to wait until she gets the body back to the morgue. Let's visit the victim's room.'

George followed Whitney to the reception, where they were given a key card to the room. As they headed up in the lift, George observed Whitney's demeanour – a mix of determination and weariness.

When they reached Merchant's room, they donned their gloves with practised ease. 'Right, you take the bathroom. I'll take the bedroom,' Whitney directed.

George entered the bathroom and meticulously examined the area, her eyes scanning for any possible clue. Finding only some vitamin pills and paracetamol, she returned to the bedroom. 'There's nothing in there of note. No insulin, so we can assume that he's not a diabetic. Have you discovered anything?'

Whitney frowned, thoughtfully. 'It's what isn't here that's worth considering. Again, there's no laptop. The fact that laptops were taken from two of the murders indicates that the murderer wants to see the victims' academic work.'

'But why wasn't Hargrove's laptop taken?'

'That's what we need to find out. Mind you, the laptops aren't going to be much use unless the person who took them knows the passwords. Although if it's someone who's familiar with the victims, they possibly—' Whitney's phone rang, interrupting her musing. 'Hello... Yes, Brian... Okay, thanks.' Whitney ended the call.

'What is it?' George asked.

'Someone's been seen in the vicinity of each of the victims' rooms. Brian is sending us their photo.'

George leant in slightly as Whitney's phone pinged and her friend opened the message, showing the photo. She immediately recognised the person. 'Oh,' she said, surprise in her voice, 'that's Emily Davies, the postgrad who's been helping organise the conference.'

'You're right. I'll ring Brian back.'

Whitney pressed the keys on her phone and put the call on speaker.

'Guv,' Brian said, answering the call after only one ring.

'We know the woman in the photo. It's Emily Davies. She's one of the conference organisers. Get the team to look into her pronto.'

'Will do, guv.' He paused a moment. 'Hang on...'

'What is it?' Whitney asked when he'd been silent for a few seconds.

'It seems that Merchant left the building and went into the grounds at ten-thirty last night. It's on the CCTV footage.'

'How did you find out? I haven't yet asked for last night's CCTV,' Whitney said, echoing George's thought.

'Frank phoned the conference centre and requested it,' Brian said.

'Ah, well, good work,' Whitney acknowledged, her voice carrying a note of approval. 'We'll be in touch. Let me know if you discover anything else.'

'Yes, guv.'

She ended the call and placed the phone into her pocket. 'We need to speak to the delegates, but in the meantime, I've been thinking that we should let the conference continue for now.'

A twinge of concern coursed through George. 'Delegates may not wish to continue with the conference when there are three dead bodies.'

'First of all, they might not know yet that we have three bodies. And secondly, it's better than hanging around all day, waiting for us to question them all, which is the alternative,' Whitney concluded, her voice trailing off.

'In that case, if we explain it to them, then they may very well agree.'

TWENTY-ONE

Friday

'We'll stop off at reception on the way to speaking to the delegates, to let them know what's going on,' Whitney said to George, her stride purposeful as they headed back into the conference centre.

'Good plan.' George nodded in agreement. 'What about Emily Davies?'

'We'll take her back to the station for questioning, but until that time we'll treat her in the same way as the rest of the people here. It could be a coincidence that she was in the vicinity of each victim but if it isn't we need to tread carefully.'

Whitney's strategic thinking always impressed George, who nodded in agreement, her eyes scanning their surroundings, always alert. It would be best to get Emily Davies away from these surroundings where she clearly felt comfortable and question her in an official environment.

They approached the desk where the manager was standing. 'Good morning, Janalyn,' Whitney greeted. 'We'd like a quick word, if we may.'

'Yes, of course,' Janalyn replied, her posture stiffening slightly, before glancing quickly at the receptionist she'd been conversing with.

The woman walked around to meet them, her movements betraying a hint of nervousness.

'We'll talk over there,' Whitney said, gesturing to a quiet corner in the foyer.

They headed over in silence.

'I understand we have another death. That makes three,' Janalyn said the moment they'd stopped walking. Her face was etched with worry.

'Yes,' Whitney confirmed. 'The pathologist is at the scene. We're treating all three deaths as suspicious, as you're no doubt aware.'

The manager anxiously glanced around the foyer, as if fearing eavesdroppers. 'I haven't been told officially, but had come to that conclusion because of your presence.'

'We haven't yet announced to the delegates that there's been a third death, but we have had the organisers ensure that everyone stays in the main conference room,' Whitney responded.

George continued analysing Janalyn's body language carefully for any signs of hesitance or deceit. Although it appeared likely the murderer was an academic, it would be foolish of them to discount staff members.

'Is there anything you want me to do?' the woman asked, her hands clasping and unclasping as she spoke.

'No. But don't mention any of this if you receive phone calls or visits from the media. Although we haven't yet informed the press of the deaths, these things do have a way of getting out. Also, please make sure that you and your staff remain silent. If you're asked, say that you don't know what's going on,' Whitney instructed firmly, leaving no room for doubt as to what was expected. Controlling the narrative in situations like this was paramount.

'Yes, that's fine. I can do that. Now, what about the conference?' Janalyn asked, betraying a hint of relief at having clear instructions and some of the responsibility lifted from her shoulders.

'At the moment, we're letting it continue. I don't want anyone to leave, so they might as well do something to keep them occupied. The plan is for everyone to be questioned, but I need the rest of my team here before that can happen. In the meantime, please ask your staff to stay on alert in case anyone tries to leave. What security do you have here?' Whitney asked.

'We have two security men,' the manager explained.

George raised an eyebrow. 'I haven't seen any.'

'That's because they keep a low profile, but we do keep an eye on proceedings. To be honest, in a place like this, we don't usually get any trouble. Maybe in the bar if someone's had too much to drink of an evening, but other than that, it's usually fine,' the manager continued.

'If you can ask them to stand at the entrances to ensure people don't leave, that would be a great help. Although, we already have officers here to assist. How many other conferences are going on at the moment?' Whitney asked.

'Fortunately, this is the only one. We had two on Monday and Tuesday, but that was it,' the manager replied.

George gave a silent sigh of relief. This information would seem to narrow down their investigation to the current conference attendees. Although it was unlikely, it was always a possibility that a delegate from another conference was responsible for the murders.

'And all delegates who attended those have left, I take it?' Whitney clarified.

'Yes, that's correct.'

'And what about your employees? Have the same staff been on all week? Let's start with your cleaners,' Whitney pressed on.

Considering their unfettered access keys to all parts of the centre, it was worth a thought.

'We have a head housekeeper, Margie, who's full-time but she was off sick on Tuesday and Wednesday. Other than that, all of our cleaners are part-time. We have different ones in each day.'

'What about catering?' Whitney asked.

'We have a small team in the kitchen, all of whom are full-time. There's the chef, the sous-chef, and four others. It's a small kitchen.'

'Okay, we will need to speak to them at some stage,' Whitney stated.

'Of course, but they don't ever go into the accommodation area and would stand out if they did. The kitchen is their domain,' Janalyn said.

'They will still be questioned at some point. For now, I'm going to let the delegates know that the conference is going to continue, but they are to stay where they are and we will be back later to question them. Thank you for your help,' Whitney said.

The manager turned and headed back to the reception desk.

Once she was out of earshot, George turned to Whitney, her brow furrowed in concern. 'Is it wise explaining everything to her? The more people who know our intentions, the more likely it is that the delegates will find out. We don't want anyone to try to slip away if they know they're going to be questioned.'

'I think it's our only option. Everyone has to know that the conference will go ahead, and that no one is allowed to leave. Also that we'll be collecting their contact details.'

'I understand,' George said. 'It's not ideal but, on reflection, it's probably the best way to proceed.'

As they headed towards the conference room, Whitney's phone rang, and she deftly pulled it out of her pocket. 'It's Ellie. I'll put her on speaker. Hello, Ellie, have you got anything for me?' Whitney asked. 'George is with me.'

'I don't know if this is going to help, guv, but when I was researching into Emily Davies, I discovered a paper that she'd recently published criticising Hargrove's Death's Shadow theory.'

Whitney's expression shifted to one of surprise and interest, and George couldn't help but mirror it.

'That's interesting,' George said. 'Where was it published? I don't believe I've seen it in any of the premier publications.'

'It's in a university research journal,' Ellie replied.

'That makes sense. It's unusual for an undergraduate to have their papers published. Please could you send me the link; I'd like to read it,' George asked the officer.

'Yes, sure. I'll send it shortly.'

'Thanks, Ellie,' Whitney said. 'Continue looking into Davies and ask Brian to contact uniform and send two uniformed officers here immediately.'

'I thought you've already got officers on the scene, guv?' Ellie replied.

'We have, but I need them to act as security to ensure no one leaves. The additional officers are to take Emily Davies to the station, where she'll be questioned.'

'Okay, guv. Leave it with me.'

Ending the call, Whitney turned to George. 'Well, there's a turn-up for the books. What do you make of Emily Davies publishing a paper criticising Hargrove?'

'Until I've seen the publication, I'm unable to comment. If it's a student journal that gets little or no attention, then her views wouldn't have had much impact. However, the fact that she is critical of the theory is something to pursue when we question her.'

'I agree. But first, we'll inform the delegates about the deaths and what's happening. They'll be informed that anyone attempting to leave will be arrested for obstruction of justice.'

'I thought we weren't going to be that fierce? That we were keeping it more low-key.'

'We were, but with hindsight and knowing that it's all going to leak soon, we should be stricter,' Whitney confirmed, her voice steady and resolved. 'I think it's the only way.'

'You're not concerned it might prompt the murderer to make their escape?'

'It would be foolish for them to do a runner because it would automatically point the finger of guilt at them.'

'True,' George agreed.

They walked into the conference room, which was buzzing with vibrant chatter but the moment George and Whitney climbed the steps onto the stage, the room went eerily silent. The delegates' expressions were a vivid tapestry of emotions – from burning curiosity to palpable apprehension, tinged with an undercurrent of ominous foreboding.

'Good morning. I'm Detective Chief Inspector Walker from Lenchester CID, and this is Dr Georgina Cavendish, who I'm sure some of you already know, or at least recognise.' George stood beside Whitney as she continued, scanning the room for any unusual reactions. 'You may or may not realise that there have been three deaths this week at the conference centre, and we are now treating them all as suspicious,' Whitney announced.

'What's that got to do with us?' a man called out from one of the front rows.

Whitney looked at him and arched an eyebrow. 'Every person here will be questioned by my officers. We want to know anything that you may or may not have witnessed, either knowingly or without realising.'

'When can we leave?' another delegate called out.

'The conference doesn't officially end until this afternoon,' Whitney said, with a dismissive wave of her hand. 'You have all arranged to be here until then, so for now, the conference will continue. This morning, you will have the planned presentation, and a team of officers will be here to interview you later. A word of warning... please don't attempt to leave the premises. There are uniformed officers in the grounds, alongside the conference centre's security officers, all of whom will stop you. Anyone who does try to leave will be arrested and taken to the station in Lenchester for questioning.'

'That's not fair,' a woman towards the rear of the conference room shouted out.

'That may be your opinion, but this is the most efficient way for us to conduct our investigation. Now, if you've got nothing to hide, which I'm sure you haven't, I suggest you sit back and enjoy the morning's session.'

Whitney's firm stance indicated she was not open to negotiation. George admired her colleague's resolve, knowing the importance of maintaining control in such a delicate situation, especially as they were dealing with often sensitive academics.

They left the stage, and the moment they were out of the room, they heard the place erupt in loud conversations.

Whitney turned to George and grinned. 'Well, that certainly made an impact. But at least they know. I want to confirm with the security staff and our officers that they're not to let anyone out, and then we'll return to the station to interview Emily Davies.'

As they exited, George pondered over the delegates' reactions. If the killer was among them, which was most likely, were they feeling the pressure? She imagined so. Either that, or they were enjoying the chaos they'd caused.

TWENTY-TWO

Sitting among the sea of stunned faces, a rush of exhilaration courses through me. My eyes scan the conference room, a faint smirk playing at the corners of my mouth.

They have no idea.

I lean back in my chair, feigning the same shock and confusion that's on the faces around me and joining in the indignant chatter that erupted the moment the police officer and the full-of-academic-self-importance Dr Cavendish left.

Three murders, all tied to this conference, and yet it's obvious they are clueless as to who's the real culprit. Of course they are, because I have more intelligence in my little finger than they have between them.

I cross my arms in a gesture of nonchalance. The drama unfolding before me is almost theatrical and the tension palpable in the air.

The fact that Merchant's demise wasn't part of my initial plan adds an element of serendipity to my scheme. It was a fortunate twist of fate that I overheard that conversation between him and Jenkins.

Merchant was a liability, a loose cannon who could have

unravelled everything. His knowledge of Hargrove's theory, his connections with Jenkins and McDonnell – it was all too risky. He had to be silenced.

Of course, McDonnell, who I had hoped to frame, might now have an alibi. If he does, it could complicate matters, but it won't derail my plans. No one suspects me, the quiet observer, the academic in the shadows.

My thoughts drift to the future, to the day when I stand on a stage like the one in front of me, basking in the glory of my intellect.

I tap my fingers on the table rhythmically, a silent tune that only I understand. My work will redefine the understanding of serial killers. It's not just about academic recognition – it's about legacy, about etching my name into the annals of history.

As the room buzzes with whispered conversations and anxious speculation, I sit, motionless, a predator amongst the oblivious prey.

A shiver of excitement runs down my spine.

They are all pawns in my grand design – mere stepping stones to my ultimate ascension.

One day soon, it will be me on that podium, receiving the adulation I rightfully deserve.

And nobody, absolutely nobody, will stand in my way.

TWENTY-THREE

Friday

Whitney and Brian entered the interview room, leaving George to head into the observation room as usual. Inside, Emily Davies sat at the table, her arms resting stiffly in her lap. Her wide eyes betrayed a mix of fear and defiance.

'Thank you for coming in, Emily,' Whitney said, taking a seat opposite her. She noted Emily's tense posture, the knuckles whitening as she gripped her own arms.

'I was made to come here,' Emily retorted, her voice tinged with resentment. 'Why? Have you brought everyone in?'

'We'd like to ask you a few questions,' Whitney began. 'It's easier to do it here at the station rather than in the hustle and bustle of the conference centre.'

'But I'm meant to be working,' Emily protested, her frustration evident in the way her brows knitted together. 'You know that. I have to make sure everything's running smoothly. That's part of my job. Otherwise, I don't get to watch the conference presentations.'

Whitney maintained her composure, despite Emily's

growing agitation. 'The sooner we get on with our interview, the sooner you can get back there,' she replied, giving Brian a subtle nod to start the recording equipment.

'Interview on Friday, fifteenth of March. Those present: Detective Chief Inspector Walker, Detective Sergeant Chapman, and... please state your name for the recording,' Brian instructed.

'Emily Constance Davies,' the woman responded, her voice quieter now, almost a whisper.

'Right, Emily,' Whitney continued, pulling out some printouts from a folder. 'We'd like to show you some stills from the CCTV cameras in the accommodation area of the conference centre.' She slid a photocopied screenshot across the table towards Emily, who hesitantly drew it closer, her eyes staring at the image. 'This first one is you outside Jonathan Hargrove's room, around lunchtime on the day that he died.'

'Yes, that's me,' Emily admitted, her fingers tracing the edge of the paper nervously.

'What were you doing there?' Whitney asked, staring at Emily, trying to read any telltale signs in her expression.

'I've already answered that,' Emily said, a hint of defensiveness creeping into her voice. 'That's when I found him dead. I went up there to deliver some papers.'

'What were these papers?' Whitney probed.

A flicker of uncertainty crossed Emily's face. 'They were papers relating to the conference. He wanted to know more about other speakers and what they were presenting. I was given the documents by one of the conference organisers.'

'Can you remember who gave them to you?' Whitney asked, her instincts telling her there was more to Emily's story than she was letting on.

'I can't, no. I'm sorry,' Emily replied, her shoulders slumping slightly.

'Okay, let's move on,' Whitney said, her mind already racing ahead, piecing together the puzzle. 'Take a look at this one.' She carefully slid another sheet across the table. 'This is you near Valerie Jenkins' room on the morning of the day she too was found dead. What were you doing there?'

Emily glanced at the photo, a hint of surprise flickering in her eyes and a slight widening of her pupils. 'I had a message to go up there because Valerie wanted to speak to me about a paper she was writing. She knew that I was interested in the Death's Shadow theory as well.'

'Which part of the theory is particularly interesting to you?' Whitney asked, leaning forwards slightly. She watched Emily's body language closely, with the intention of gauging the sincerity behind the woman's words.

'Well, I was more interested in critiquing what Professor Hargrove had outlined in his,' Emily began, her voice wavering slightly. Her hands had subtly shifted, her fingers now intertwining nervously.

'I'd like to find out what her issues are with the theory. Start by asking what she thinks about its internal consistency,' George suggested.

'So, if that's the case, explain what you think about its internal consistency,' Whitney asked, resting her arms on the table.

Emily's eyes opened wide, a mixture of surprise and apprehension. 'You're aware of the theory?'

'Of course I am. When investigating someone's death, I make sure to know everything about them,' Whitney responded with a calm confidence. She was happy that George could feed her anything she needed to know for Emily Davies to be convinced of her knowledge.

Emily hesitated. 'Well... I have the same views as Valerie Jenkins, that the concept of the shadow self has to be aligned with other psychological theories.'

Inside, Whitney was weighing up Emily's reactions, trying

to discern whether she was just a nervous academic or something more.

'Can you be a bit more specific?' she urged, sensing a possible crack in Emily's composed exterior.

Emily faltered, glancing away for a moment before returning to look at Whitney. 'Well, you could ask yourself, you know, whether it's a completely new psychological phenomenon that he was pointing out, or whether it's simply a subset of another psychological condition, like... um... dissociative identity. I don't believe that Hargrove gave that specific attention.'

'What were other issues you found?' Whitney continued, keeping her voice steady but insistent.

Emily took a deep breath, visibly trying to collect her thoughts. 'Um—'

'Well, for example, is it easy to put this theory into practice if you're working as a psychologist?' Whitney asked.

'Well, no, I suppose it's more a theoretical statement. It would be hard for anyone to identify that someone's shadow self was at play,' Emily concluded, her voice barely more than a whisper.

Whitney nodded slowly. 'I see. So, you were discussing these shortcomings with Valerie Jenkins?'

'I was planning to. I've already mentioned some of them in a paper I wrote,' Emily admitted, a tinge of defensiveness creeping into her voice.

'Yes, we know about that. It was published in a student journal,' Whitney said, continuing to watch Emily's reaction closely.

'You know that, too?' Emily's jaw tensed.

'Of course. Right, so returning to my previous questions. You were near Valerie Jenkins' room, close to the time when she was murdered. Is that correct?'

'Yes, but it was just a coincidence.'

'Did you actually speak to her?'

'No, because I was called back to the conference. I didn't actually meet up with her in the end,' Emily finished.

Whitney's mind churned. She exchanged a brief, knowing glance with Brian, silently communicating their shared scepticism. There was more to Emily's story than she was letting on, and Whitney was determined to uncover it.

Whitney laid out another CCTV image before Emily. 'Okay, here's another shot from the CCTV footage from yesterday. Here you are, close to Toby Merchant's room. What were you doing there?'

'There was a message left for me at reception to go up to his room.' Emily's voice wavered slightly, a hint of uncertainty creeping in. 'He wanted to give me something. I don't know what it was.'

'Who left you the message?' Whitney asked, scrutinising Emily's face for any sign of deceit. Although George was the expert, she was also able to discern when a suspect was trying to pull the wool over their eyes.

'I don't know, it was just on reception,' Emily replied, screwing up her eyes for a moment.

'Do you often get messages left at reception?' Whitney pushed. The woman's answers were weakening by the second.

'I have done, from various people,' Emily responded, but her voice lacked conviction.

'Do you still have this message?' Whitney watched Emily's discomfort grow.

'I threw it away,' she said.

'You threw it away,' Whitney repeated, disbelief in her tone. 'Where?'

A discarded message was most convenient.

'In one of the bins and then I headed up to the room. I knocked on the door, and there was no one there.'

'So, you didn't actually see Toby Merchant?'

Something wasn't adding up.

'No,' Emily replied, a bit too quickly for Whitney's liking.

'What time was it when you went up to his room?' Whitney continued.

'Um... It was after dinner, so maybe around eight-thirty. I don't know exactly.'

'You were still working then? That's late.'

'I'm on duty until everybody has gone upstairs and left the conference area. Look, I got the message, went up there to see what he wanted. When he wasn't there, I came down. That's all. You have to believe me.'

'Did you go out into the grounds at all last night?' Whitney asked, moving the conversation on.

Emily blushed.

Were they on to something?

'You've hit the nail there. Keep going,' George said, confirming Whitney's own thoughts.

'Emily, answer the question,' Whitney insisted.

'Yes, I did. I went out for some fresh air.'

'On your own?' Whitney asked, conscious of Emily avoiding direct eye contact.

'She was definitely with someone,' George observed in Whitney's ear.

'Let me answer for you, Emily. No, you weren't. Who were you with?' Whitney's question was direct, leaving little room for evasion.

There was silence for a few seconds whilst Emily peered at her lap, as if she'd find the answers there. Finally, she raised her eyes. 'I admit to going outside to meet someone, but I'm not saying who.' Emily's voice quivered.

What was she scared of?

'If it was perfectly innocent, then there's no reason for you not to tell us,' Whitney countered, not prepared to let the woman off that easily.

Emily bit down on her bottom lip, her internal struggle clear. 'I can't say anything, I can't. It's nothing to do with Toby Merchant, you have to believe me. I promise. But I can't tell you.'

She pulled a tissue out and wiped away the tears that were glistening in her eyes.

Was it for real, or was she simply a bloody good actress? Whatever, Whitney wouldn't be letting her off that easily. She'd learnt her lesson many years ago not to take things at face value.

'Emily, it's going to come out sooner or later. It would be much easier on you if you tell us who you were meeting. Then we can eliminate you from our enquiries,' Whitney reasoned.

'It's not like that,' Emily said, sniffing. She sat upright in her chair, her expression now resolute. 'I'm not saying anything else until I have a solicitor here.'

Whitney inwardly groaned. This could significantly slow things down. 'Okay. Phone your solicitor. You can stay here until they arrive.'

'Why can't I go?' Emily sounded desperate.

'Put it this way, you're not under arrest, but you will be if you try to leave,' Whitney stated firmly, leaving no room for misunderstanding. She was determined to get to the bottom of this, no matter how complex it became.

TWENTY-FOUR

Friday

'Come on, we'll go back to the incident room,' Whitney said after leaving Emily Davies alone in the interview room. She motioned for Brian and George to follow her through the station. She rubbed her forehead briefly as they walked. 'If she won't tell us, we have to try and discover who she was with ourselves. We need to check the CCTV footage to see if we can see her outside.' Whitney's stride was purposeful, her mind whirring with thoughts.

'Right, listen up, everyone,' she began once they'd walked into the room, commanding the attention of her team. 'We've got Emily Davies downstairs. She's now demanded to see a solicitor, so we've left her there. I want to have a look at the CCTV footage to see if we can spot her going out into the grounds, which she admitted she did.'

'I've got the footage from last night, guv,' Frank said. 'It came over a while ago. The camera at the entrance is focused on the door and out into the grounds. I imagine she went out the front door; we can check there first.'

'Good. Put it up on the big screen so we can all have a look.'

As the CCTV footage appeared, Whitney took a step forward her eyes narrowing as she scrutinised the images. 'There she is,' Brian pointed out, his finger jabbing towards the rolling footage where Emily had just walked into shot.

'Right, so she went outside alone. Did she go out before Merchant or after?' Whitney pondered aloud, her mind visibly racing through the possibilities.

The team watched intently as the footage continued. The time stamp accelerated on at triple speed, and about half an hour later, Toby Merchant was seen leaving. 'Okay, so she goes outside at about ten-fifteen, closely followed by him at around ten-forty-five. But we can't see where they're headed, if indeed they went in the same direction,' Whitney observed, frustrated.

'The cameras don't go that far, guv, so that's all we've got,' Frank added, sounding equally annoyed.

'Well, that's a pain in the arse. Nobody else has gone outside by the looks of this, which totally contradicts Emily Davies' account,' Whitney remarked, crossing her arms in a mix of contemplation and irritation.

'Not that we've seen. Is there another way that somebody could go outside without being seen?' Doug asked.

Whitney turned to George, seeking her input. 'Is it possible? You know the place better than the rest of us.'

'There could be a staff entrance at the back.'

Whitney nodded, considering this new information. 'Have you actually seen this entrance?'

'Well, I was looking around one time while I was waiting for a session to start and saw a couple of people coming through from the back wearing outdoor coats,' George recalled. 'There must be several ways in and out because of fire regulations. But we don't have CCTV footage from any of the staff areas.'

'Do you think it's a member of staff who did this?' Frank

questioned, leaning back in his chair, his expression one of scepticism.

'Not necessarily,' George reasoned. 'I can't imagine it's kept securely locked, from the inside anyway, so anyone could easily go through that way.'

Whitney considered this angle. 'Okay, so what we're saying is that someone can go outside without being spotted on the cameras, providing they know where these entrances are.'

'Where does that put Emily Davies?' Meena asked, her brow furrowed in concentration. 'If she's the murderer, why would she have gone outside in full view of the cameras? Also, wouldn't she have made sure not to be seen in the vicinity of the victims' rooms?'

'Do you think she's being set up?' Frank speculated, his eyes flicking from face to face.

'Possibly. Or she actually is our killer and not very adept at covering her tracks,' Whitney replied.

'What's her motive?' Frank asked.

'That's for us to find out,' Whitney mused, her eyes relishing the challenge of unravelling the mystery. 'But we can't pursue that until her solicitor has arrived. What time did she go back inside?'

Frank fast-forwarded the footage, stopping when the woman appeared. 'There she is and it's eleven-fifteen.'

Whitney's phone rang, and she pulled it out of her pocket. It was Claire. 'Morning, Claire, what have you got for me?'

'I believe it's insulin poisoning again, and I'm waiting for the toxicology results. I found the entry point. Also, the death occurred between eleven p.m. and two a.m.'

'Right, okay, thanks, Claire, that's really useful.' She ended the call. 'Okay, we've got a time of death between eleven and two. I want to speak to Emily Davies again. Because she had enough time to kill Merchant and get back inside.'

'But her solicitor's not here,' Brian said.

'We'll call it an unofficial chat. She doesn't have to answer our questions, but if we tell her what we know, she might be prepared to. The rest of you carry on with your work whilst Brian, George, and I go back to speak to her.'

They left and walked down the corridor. 'I'm not really happy about this, guv,' Brian said.

'I get it. She's asked for a solicitor and what we're doing is against procedure. I'll make it perfectly clear that she's under no obligation to answer our questions. I promise that it will be okay,' Whitney reassured him confidently, despite the niggle at the back of her mind.

'Okay. If you're sure it's not going to come back and bite us on the bum,' Brian said with a resigned shrug.

They left George in the observation area and went into the room. Emily Davies was sitting upright, blankly staring ahead.

'Emily, I know your solicitor hasn't arrived, but I want another few words with you. You do not need to answer any of my questions, but I want to tell you what we've discovered, in case it makes a difference to you wanting to wait for your representation.'

Emily sat with her arms crossed, her eyes flitting around the room, avoiding Whitney's. 'Okay,' she said hesitatingly, her voice barely above a whisper.

'Thank you. We know that you went outside half an hour before Toby Merchant. There's nobody else on the CCTV footage leaving the premises, so it's all pointing to you going to meet him. Now, if you tell us something that can help our enquiries, the Crown Prosecution Service might go easy on you. Why don't you want to admit what happened between the two of you?'

As Whitney spoke, Emily's eyes widened, and her mouth fell open slightly. She recoiled, as if the words had physically struck her.

'I'll tell you everything, but I had nothing to do with his

death, I promise. It wasn't me.' Her hands unfolded and her eyes, now locked onto Whitney's, conveyed a desperate plea for belief.

'Okay.' Whitney observed the shift in Emily's demeanour. 'Does this mean you're happy to give us a statement and that we can record it?'

Emily nodded firmly, taking a deep breath as if to steady herself. 'Yes. I want to clear this up.' There was a resolve in her voice that wasn't there before.

'Even though your solicitor isn't here?' Whitney asked, wanting to make doubly sure that it wouldn't come back to haunt her.

'Yes. I want you to know everything because I didn't kill him. I didn't kill anyone.'

'Okay, Brian, restart the tape. Right, over to you, Emily. You tell us everything.'

'I do have an alibi. Yes, I was outside, possibly when Toby Merchant was killed, but I'd actually gone to meet another delegate from the conference.' Emily's hands fidgeted with the edge of her shirt.

'Why outside and not inside?' Whitney probed further, scrutinising Emily's nervous demeanour.

Emily sucked in a breath, her shoulders tensing up. 'We've been seeing each other on the side.'

Oh. That made more sense.

'Who is this person?' Whitney asked.

'They're married. That's why I couldn't say anything because I don't want to get them in trouble.' Emily's voice was barely above a whisper, her fingers now intertwined tightly in her lap.

'Look, Emily, you're going to have to tell us. We can be discreet – it doesn't have to come out, but we will need them to be your alibi.'

'Okay, I understand,' she said, her voice steadier now. 'It's

Dr Miranda Rathbone. She's one of the delegates here. We met outside at around a quarter past ten and we went for a walk in the grounds. We were only out for an hour. I got back to my room before eleven-thirty.' Her eyes flickered to the side, recalling the events.

'Okay, and so you're saying that all you did was walk around for an hour?'

'There are some benches a bit further out in the grounds, and we sat on one of those for a while chatting.' Emily's hands gestured vaguely, mimicking the act of sitting.

'Did anyone see you go back into the conference centre?'

'Not that I know of. I didn't see anyone until I got to my room, and there was somebody else in the corridor. I couldn't tell you who that was, though.' Emily shrugged slightly, looking uncertain.

'We picked you up going inside on the CCTV footage, but you were alone. Where was Dr Rathbone?'

'We didn't want to be seen together so I think that Miranda used the French windows in the main conference room to come out to meet me and to go back inside.' Emily's eyebrows furrowed, as if trying to piece together the logic.

'Did you actually witness Dr Rathbone come outside?' Whitney asked.

'Yes, I did.'

'And go back through the French windows?'

'Yes. We parted company a little way from the entrance, but I was still able to see her walk over to the doors and go inside.'

'Aren't they usually kept locked?' Whitney asked.

'Yes, but Miranda opened the door from the inside. There's no key.'

'How long have you been seeing Dr Rathbone?'

'Not long... Just a couple of months.' Emily's voice wavered, her hands trembling.

'How did you meet?'

'I attended one of her lectures. She's from my university. I stayed behind after to talk to her, and we got on and we ended up going for coffee. It developed from there.'

Whitney nodded thoughtfully, filing away this detail. 'I see. Is that why you came to the conference? Because of her?'

'It was, in part, yes.'

'Have you been meeting up with her every day during the conference?'

Emily's discomfort was palpable, and Whitney felt a twinge of sympathy as she pursued the line of questioning.

'When we can. We can't let anyone know that we're with each other, though.'

'Thank you for explaining. We'll speak to Dr Rathbone to confirm your alibi.'

'Okay, but please don't tell anyone else... and please tell her that I only confessed to seeing her because there was nothing else I could do.' Emily's plea tugged at Whitney's sense of duty.

'Don't worry, it will be kept quiet if it's not something that's needed for the investigation. To confirm, you've only been seeing each other for a few months?'

'Yes, coming up for three.'

'You can stay here until we get to confirm your alibi.'

'Do I still need my solicitor?' Emily asked.

'That's up to you, but I wouldn't cancel them yet,' Whitney said decisively, as she stood up.

They left the room and met up with George in the corridor.

'Well, that wasn't what I expected,' Brian said, after closing the door behind him.

'Yes. We need to get hold of this Dr Rathbone. George, do you know her?'

'No. But that's hardly surprising. It's a large conference and I don't know everyone. In particular, I'm not familiar with anyone from the university Emily and Dr Rathbone attend.'

'We need to get back to the conference centre to confirm this alibi. Because if Emily's in the clear we're back to square one.'

TWENTY-FIVE

Friday

'We'll get Dr Rathbone out of the conference room,' Whitney said, her voice low and urgent as they went in through the entrance. 'I don't want anyone to be alerted that we're back.'

George scanned the area meticulously, her keen eyes missing nothing. There were police in the grounds and the security was on the door, so no one would have been able to get out. They walked over to the reception desk, to where Wayne was at the desk.

'I'd like you to ask one of the conference organisers to call out Dr Rathbone. Don't say what it's about, though,' Whitney instructed.

'Shall I say there's a call in reception for her?' Wayne asked, his brow furrowed slightly.

'Do you know her?' Whitney asked, her curiosity sounding piqued.

'Yes, I believe so. There have been messages for her during the conference. I'll call one of the organisers and ask them to fetch her.'

'And where can we go to interview her?'

'All the breakout rooms are free, but I'd suggest using number five because it's small and out of the way.'

'Perfect. We don't want any unnecessary attention.'

'Understood,' Wayne said, picking up the phone.

In the breakout room they found a large oblong table, surrounded by chairs, with a whiteboard at one end and a TV screen at the other. In the middle of the table was an empty jug with glasses.

'I'm not sure whether I want this Dr Rathbone to give Emily Davies an alibi or not,' Whitney mused aloud, her fingers tapping on the tabletop, betraying her impatience.

'I imagine you'd prefer not,' George said. 'Because without an alibi, she's our prime suspect and that moves the case forward.'

'You can see where I'm coming from, then? If Davies has an alibi, then we have three deaths and no clue as to who the killer is.'

'I would disagree that we haven't got anywhere,' George replied. 'We've established that the killings are most likely linked to the Death's Shadow theory, which our victims were all either working on or criticising.'

Whitney sighed. 'I suppose you're right. Unless we've got the wrong end of the stick and are barking up the wrong tree, to quote two clichés in succession, which is almost as bad as believing in coincidences.' A faint smile crept onto her lips.

A light tap on the door drew them away from the conversation. In walked a woman who looked to be in her early fifties with dark auburn hair that was cut into a short bob. A light smattering of freckles were dotted across her nose.

'I was asked to come here. I'm Miranda Rathbone,' the woman said with trepidation in her voice.

'Ah, please come in, Dr Rathbone. I'm DCI Walker from Lenchester CID and this is Dr Cavendish.'

The woman's shoulders tensed and she looked at George and back to Whitney.

'Yes, I saw you this morning when you spoke to us. Is there a problem? Why have you asked me here?'

'Please take a seat, Dr Rathbone,' Whitney said.

'Call me Miranda,' the woman said, giving a nervous smile.

They all pulled out a chair from around the table and sat.

'I'm afraid what we wish to ask you is a little delicate,' Whitney said gently. 'But it's imperative we do.'

'Delicate?' The academic appeared confused.

'Yes, it's about Emily Davies.'

'Oh.' Rathbone pressed her lips together and averted her eyes.

She clearly understood what was about to be disclosed and wasn't happy about it.

'Please, could you confirm – and we don't intend for this to go elsewhere unless it is evidence – that you and Emily have been seeing each other?' Whitney asked, keeping her eyes focused on the woman.

'Umm... yes. But please, it mustn't become public knowledge. It's...' Her voice fell away.

'We understand. Emily has given you as an alibi for last night. Is it correct that you met one another in the grounds of the centre last night?' Whitney continued.

The woman nodded. 'Yes,' she said softly.

'Thank you. What time did you leave each other?'

'I'm not sure exactly, possibly around eleven? It wouldn't have been much later than that because I had arranged to phone my husband at eleven-fifteen.'

'That's late for a phone call,' George said.

'He's a night bird. We both are,' Rathbone said with a shrug.

'When you went to meet with Emily, you didn't use the front door, did you?' Whitney asked, jotting down a few notes in her pad.

'No, I used the French windows in the conference room.'

'Why was that?' George asked.

'For secrecy. I thought going out and back in that way, we wouldn't be seen.'

'But wouldn't going out the same entrance at separate times have had the same outcome?' George pushed.

'Maybe. Just call it the two of us being extra cautious. Does it matter?'

'No, I suppose not. Did you know there's no CCTV covering where you exited?' Whitney asked.

'Umm... No. I didn't. But avoiding cameras wasn't my intention. It was to ensure other delegates didn't spot Emily and me together. I'm married,' she added, a blush creeping up her cheeks.

'We're not here to discuss that,' Whitney said, giving a dismissive wave of her hand. 'You're probably aware that a third person has died at the hotel. Dr Toby Merchant, Jonathan Hargrove's research assistant. Do you know him?' Whitney asked.

'Not by name, no.' Rathbone shook her head.

'I'll show you a photo.' Whitney took out her phone, pulled up an image, and showed it to her.

Rathbone nodded slowly. 'Ah... Yes... he does look vaguely familiar. I probably saw him at the conference. And he's now dead? That's awful.'

'Yes, it is. Think carefully, Miranda,' Whitney said in an encouraging tone. 'Do you remember seeing him when you went outside to meet Emily last night? Around ten-forty-five or so.'

Rathbone appeared thoughtful and George stared directly at the woman, analysing her body language in order to discern the accuracy of her responses.

'I don't believe so, but to be honest I can't be sure. Emily and I walked around, and then sat on one of the benches outside. After that we went back inside.'

That certainly matched Emily Davies' account. But there was something not quite right. George stared more closely at Rathbone, sensing there was something on her mind, but she couldn't pinpoint what it was.

'Did you go to Jonathan Hargrove's lecture on Sunday?' George asked.

'Yes, I did.'

'What are your views about his theory? Are they the same as Emily's?'

'Is this related to why he died?' Rathbone asked.

'No, I was just curious,' George said, sensing that was the right approach in order to elicit more from the woman.

'I won't deny it's caused waves in the academic community, but... Well...' She paused.

'What is it?' Whitney asked.

'Emily has much stronger opinions on it than I do. She wrote a critique on it for our university's student research journal.'

'Yes, we're aware of that,' Whitney said.

'Good,' Rathbone said, relief in her voice. 'Is there anything else I can help you with?'

'Not for the moment, but please don't mention our conversation to anyone. We'll be interviewing all delegates shortly, once my team has arrived,' Whitney said.

'Of course, I understand,' Rathbone said. She glanced briefly towards the door, clearly anxious to leave. 'And you won't let anyone find out about Emily and me? My husband's an academic, and it's a small world. If it gets back to him... it could totally ruin our family life.'

'Do you have children?' Whitney asked, gently.

Rathbone's face softened slightly, revealing a more vulnerable side. 'My husband has two children from a previous marriage who stay with us every other weekend. I love them like my own. So you can understand how difficult this situation is.'

'We do, and we appreciate your honesty,' Whitney reassured. 'The main thing is, you've given Emily an alibi.'

'Yes, although...' Rathbone hesitated.

George went on alert, her interest piqued.

'Although what?' Whitney pushed.

'Look, I shouldn't be saying this – please don't say it was me who told you,' Rathbone began, her voice lowering as if sharing a secret. 'When we headed back inside, Emily said that she'd left her scarf on the bench. She headed back towards where we came from.'

So that was it. George had known the woman had something on her mind. Now it made sense.

'Did you see Emily go back inside?' Whitney asked, her eyebrows raised in query.

'No, I'm sorry, I didn't.'

'She can't have been much longer, because she was on the CCTV footage going in,' George added.

'Okay, well, it's nothing then,' Rathbone concluded, a hint of relief in her voice as she stood up, her posture slightly more relaxed now that the questioning seemed to be over.

'Thank you for your time, Miranda,' Whitney said, giving a nod of dismissal.

Dr Rathbone left the room and George rubbed her chin thoughtfully. 'Now what?' she murmured.

'I want the rest of the team here. I'll give them a call. They can bring Emily Davies back, too, now we have her alibi. Even going back for her scarf, it would have been difficult to kill Merchant in such a short space of time.' Whitney picked up her phone and made the call. 'Brian, it's me. I want you, Meena, Doug and Frank down to interview the delegates now. Bring Emily Davies with you. She can join the others.'

Whitney ended the call and George stood up, stretching her

legs, her mind already racing ahead, thinking about the interviews to come.

'Have you planned what we're going to do if the interviews don't produce any useful information?' George asked.

'Thanks for jinxing it,' Whitney said, rolling her eyes. 'Anyway, someone will have seen something. I can feel it in my bones.'

TWENTY-SIX

Friday

'We'll divide the delegates up into groups,' Whitney said as the team gathered around her at the conference centre. 'There are about a hundred of them. We'll interview in pairs. George and me, Doug and Frank, Brian and Meena.'

'Who's going to interview which group, guv?' Frank asked.

'I was coming to that. You and Doug will speak to those who attended Hargrove's Sunday evening presentation. It's my belief that they're the most likely to have crucial information. Ask for details about the evening of the presentation and any conversations they had with Professor Hargrove themselves or that they witnessed.'

'Got it, guv,' Frank said.

'George and I will interview the organisers and panellists who might have insights into the professor's interactions and behaviour during the conference. Meena and Brian, take the rest. Ask more general questions. Find out if they noticed anything that might not have seemed important at the time but could be relevant in hindsight.'

'Yes, guv,' Brian and Meena both said.

'If anything relevant does come up, find me straight away,' Whitney continued, her hands gesturing to emphasise her points. 'We'll divide them up and use the breakout rooms. I'll ask the security staff to stand on guard at the door to make sure no one leaves. Any questions?'

'Are we to interview the whole group at one time, or further split them?' Brian asked.

'Interview them in twos and threes. It goes without saying that the interviews should be conducted in a manner that is respectful and sensitive to the fact that the delegates are here primarily for a conference, not an investigation.'

'We know that, guv. We've been doing this long enough,' Brian said, impatiently.

'Sorry. Of course you do,' Whitney said, holding up her hands apologetically. 'Right. Follow me.'

She led the way as they walked into the conference room, and down by the side of the podium. Climbing up onto the stage, she took a moment to survey the crowd, mentally preparing herself for the task ahead.

'Good afternoon, everyone. I'm sorry that this has taken so long, but thank you for your patience. The conference is now over, but we would like to speak to you all before you leave.' She paused for a moment to allow that to sink in. 'Once you've been interviewed, providing you leave your address and contact details with my officers, you're free to go. We will be dividing you up into groups. Organisers and panellists, please sit at the far end of the room. Those of you who attended Professor Hargrove's presentation on Sunday evening, sit in the middle, and the rest of you, please congregate close to the stage. You'll be interviewed in small groups. Any questions?'

'I need the loo,' someone called out.

'That's fine, you can go now, but come straight back.'

Whitney indicated towards the door. 'There's a security person on the door who will escort you. Anything else?'

As there were no further questions, she stepped down from the podium. They waited for a few minutes until the delegates had divided up into their respective groups, and then the team made a start.

Whitney and George led two of the organisers, Paul Gleeson and Mandy Lewis, into one of the breakout rooms, leaving the remaining two organisers, including Emily Davies, and the six panellists to be interviewed in due course.

'Please give me your contact details. Address and mobile number,' Whitney said once they had settled into the breakout room they'd been assigned.

'Are we going to be long?' Paul Gleeson, the younger of the two, said, after Whitney had taken down their details. 'I promised my wife I'd try and leave early. It's parents' evening at the school.'

'We'll try not to keep you too long,' Whitney said. 'Was there anything during the conference that concerned you, that perhaps you haven't thought about initially, but now, on reflection, you think was odd?' She observed them closely, looking for any signs of hesitation or discomfort, but there was nothing that put her on alert.

'I can't say that there was,' Paul Gleeson said, looking at his colleague, who agreed with him.

There was an ease to his voice. Genuine or a façade?

'Despite Professor Hargrove dying, which we thought was just an unfortunate incident, it all ran smoothly. All the sessions were well received,' Mandy Lewis added.

'I understand there were some heated exchanges during Professor Hargrove's Sunday presentation between the professor and Angus McDonnell,' Whitney said.

'That's standard,' Mandy said with a wave of her hand. 'I've witnessed much worse.'

Whitney glanced at George, who nodded in agreement.

'Did you hear any talk from the centre staff, or others, that delegates wanted to leave after they'd learnt about the deaths of Hargrove and Jenkins?'

'I didn't hear anything,' Mandy said.

'Nor me,' Paul said.

Whitney frowned. Was this normal behaviour, or did their academic discipline make them immune to being surrounded by death? Or maybe it made them even more determined to stay, out of curiosity.

'Emily Davies mentioned being left a message on reception to take something up to Toby Merchant's room yesterday. Do you know who would have left it for her?'

'It's not something we would usually do, so I don't. It certainly wasn't me,' Mandy said.

'You don't leave messages for each other?' Whitney clarified.

'No, I meant we wouldn't leave one on reception. It would be hand delivered.'

'Every time? What if it's something important?'

'Even more reason to ensure someone receives it,' Mandy confirmed.

Whitney scribbled a note in her book, her thoughts already moving ahead to the next question.

'When Emily found Professor Hargrove, she'd been on her way to his room with some papers. What do you know about that?'

'I asked her to take them,' Mandy said. 'Professor Hargrove wanted to get them sent up.'

'He asked you directly?'

'No, there was a message left on reception. Oh...' Her eyes darted from Whitney to George. 'And I just said we don't leave messages on reception. I was wrong. I should have said it doesn't happen often.'

'Was the message left specifically for you?' Whitney asked.

'Thinking back, one of the receptionists called out when I was walking past and gave it to me. My name wasn't on it.'

'Did you ask the receptionist who left the message?'

'No, because I assumed it was Professor Hargrove.'

'I see.' Whitney tried to keep her excitement hidden. Finally, they were getting somewhere. 'Emily also went to see Valerie Jenkins, but that was pre-arranged. Did any of you know about that?' She looked at each of them in turn.

'No,' they responded in unison.

There was a knock on the door, and Meena poked her head in. 'Guv, can I have a word, please?'

'Yes, of course.' Whitney stood up, a mix of anticipation and urgency in her movements. 'Excuse me.' She stepped outside into the corridor, her heart racing with the prospect of new information.

'I think we've got something,' Meena began. 'One of the conference delegates mentioned that on Monday they had to help someone go back to their room for some glucose because they were in danger of having a hypo. They'd gone all weak and sick.'

Whitney's heartbeat quickened. 'Who was it? Do you have a name?'

'Yes. It's Dr Rathbone.'

Whitney's jaw dropped open. What the...

'Dr *Miranda* Rathbone. Are you saying that she's diabetic?'

'Yes, guv.'

Bloody hell.

She'd never have guessed.

The woman deserved an Oscar after her performance earlier.

'That's excellent. Well done, Meena. Get hold of Rathbone for me. I take it she's not in the breakout room with you.' Whitney's thoughts raced ahead, considering the implications.

'No.'

'I'll see if she's in the hall, and you check with Frank and Doug – she might be with them.' Whitney's stride quickened as she moved into the main hall and scanned the whole place.

Except... she wasn't there.

Meena rushed into the hall and made a beeline for Whitney. 'She's not in with the others.'

Where the hell was she?

Surely she couldn't know what they'd just found out.

'She must have left. But how could she have done with so much security?'

'She might be in her room,' Meena suggested.

'Agreed. I want you to instruct everybody that they can go, but make sure we have their contact details. Inform security of the decision. I'll collect George and we'll look for Rathbone.'

'What if we're wrong, guv?' Meena asked, looking uncertain. 'Shouldn't we keep the delegates here until we've checked if any more of them are diabetic? The chances are at least some of them might be.'

'It would take too long to check with each delegate individually and then confirm it with their medical practitioner. Providing we have their contact details, if Rathbone turns out not to be our murderer we can still contact them,' Whitney said, hoping that she'd made the right decision.

'Yes, guv, that makes sense,' Meena replied, hurrying out of the room.

Whitney returned to the breakout room. 'We've finished the questioning for now. You're free to leave.' Whitney waited until Gleeson and Lewis had left the room before speaking. 'Rathbone's a diabetic; one of the delegates helped her after she had a hypo. Meena and I have checked, and she's not here. We need to focus on finding her; that's why I've let the other delegates go. She might still be in her room. Come on.'

They left the breakout room and hurried towards reception.

Whitney's stride was fast, her mind already racing with possibilities. 'Dr Rathbone's room, what number is it?' she called out to Wayne before they even reached the counter.

The receptionist, looking slightly flustered, quickly checked the computer. 'It's on the first floor,' he informed them. Without hesitation, Whitney and George turned and ran to the stairs, their footsteps echoing in the empty stairwell.

When they reached the room, the door was slightly open. They stepped inside and Whitney's heart sank. The room was clearly vacated – everything was packed and gone.

They raced back down to reception.

'Did you know that Miranda Rathbone has gone?' Whitney asked Wayne, her voice edged with impatience.

The receptionist's frown deepened, reflecting his confusion.

'Uh, no, I didn't,' he admitted, peering at the computer screen. 'But looking at this, I can see that she has checked out.'

Whitney's frustration grew. 'I said everyone was to stay. When did this happen?'

'I don't know, I've only just come back from a break,' the receptionist replied defensively.

'Right, who checked her out? Have a look,' Whitney demanded.

'It was the manager.'

'Fetch her.'

Wayne left the desk and went through the door at the back.

A few seconds later, Janalyn Prude appeared, her expression curious. 'Is there an issue?' she enquired, addressing Whitney and George.

'Yes, you checked out Miranda Rathbone.' Whitney's eyes fixed on her, searching for answers.

'Yes, because you'd spoken to her already,' Janalyn explained.

Whitney's internal alarm bells were ringing. She had a sinking feeling they'd missed a critical piece.

'And you didn't think to check with us?' Whitney interjected, her frustration evident in her voice.

'Well, no, because Wayne had told me earlier that you were interviewing her and Dr Rathbone said that you'd agreed to it,' Janalyn replied, seemingly oblivious to the gravity of the situation. 'I had no reason to doubt her.'

'Right. We've announced that the delegates can all leave now, so long as we've got their contact details.' Whitney's mind was racing, trying to piece together Rathbone's sudden departure and its implications for their investigation.

'Okay,' the manager said.

'Come on, George, we've got to find the woman,' she said. 'Do you have Dr Rathbone's home address on your system?' Whitney asked, turning to the receptionist.

He glanced at the manager, who nodded her assent.

'Yes, I can get it up for you,' he responded, his fingers flying over the keyboard.

'Email it to me,' Whitney instructed while pulling her phone from her pocket. 'I need to get hold of Ellie.'

'Guv?' Ellie answered on the first ring.

'Arrange backup to the address I'm about to forward to you. It's Miranda Rathbone. She's diabetic. Do some research into her. I think she's the murderer.'

TWENTY-SEVEN

Friday

'Come on, put your foot down, George. I know you want to,' Whitney urged as they drove towards Rathbone's house. 'We can't let her get away.'

George stole a glance at her partner, who was sitting upright in their car, staring intently out of the window, her fingers clutching the edge of the seat.

'I don't intend to cause an accident or be stopped for speeding, Whitney,' George said, evenly. 'Rathbone doesn't know we're on our way to her house, nor does she know that we suspect her of the crimes. She's most likely gone home, which means there's definitely no need to speed. It's not as if I have a siren to ensure people get out of my way,' George replied, sounding slightly exasperated.

'Okay, okay... I understand,' Whitney conceded with a shrug. 'It's just I want to get there quickly.'

Because that wasn't obvious.

A few minutes later, they drew up outside a large Victorian terraced house, overlooking a park, in a pleasant leafy suburb in

Rugby. George's eyes immediately were drawn to a vehicle parked outside. 'I wonder if that's Dr Rathbone's car,' she mused.

'We'll soon find out,' Whitney said, unfastening her seat belt and jumping out of the car.

They headed to the door and Whitney rang the bell.

After a short time, a slightly overweight man of around five foot eight answered. His eyebrows arched in a way that made him appear permanently surprised. He wore jeans and an open-neck checked shirt.

'Mr Rathbone?' Whitney enquired, keeping her voice professional, not wanting to give anything away at this stage.

'No, my name's Vernon Barton,' he said with a weariness that suggested he'd been asked that question on more than one occasion.

'But are you Miranda Rathbone's husband?' Whitney clarified.

'Yes, that's correct.'

'Is she here?' Whitney asked. 'I'm Detective Chief Inspector Walker from Lenchester CID, and this is my associate, Dr Cavendish.'

'No, she's not. Why, what's this about? My wife's at a conference. Has something happened to her?' A look of panic crossed his face.

'As far as we're aware, she's fine. The conference finished early and she'd already left before we could speak to her about some events that have occurred. Please can we come inside and wait?'

'What events?' he asked, a hint of suspicion in his voice.

'We'll explain more once we're inside,' Whitney assured him.

'Okay,' Barton said, stepping to the side to allow them to enter.

They headed through the small porch and turned immediately left into a large open-plan room with high ceilings and a beautiful ornate fireplace with a marble mantelpiece and an intricate floral surround. A large bay window, with heavy, deep-red curtains, cast a warm natural light across the room. George took in every detail, her mind alert to any clues that might aid their investigation.

Barton sat on one of the wing-backed chairs, and George and Whitney took a seat on a sofa facing him.

'Has Miranda told you about some unfortunate deaths that have occurred during the conference?' Whitney enquired.

Barton's eyes widened. He clearly hadn't heard.

'Deaths? No. She didn't tell me. We haven't spoken all week. Deaths... Goodness.'

'I thought she mentioned to me that she phoned you at around eleven last night. I must have been mistaken,' Whitney said, tilting her head to one side.

'We're never in contact when we're at conferences,' Barton said, with a dismissive wave. 'We're usually too busy... networking,' he replied, a slight hesitation in his voice.

Was he hiding something?

'Ah, I see,' Whitney said, exchanging a quick glance with George, who nodded slightly in understanding. 'Do you know what your wife's currently working on?'

'Yes. Serial killers,' the man replied, his voice firmer, as if comfortable now he was on safer ground.

'Have you heard of the Death's Shadow theory?' Whitney asked.

'Yes, it was put forward by Jonathan Hargrove,' Barton said. The man rolled his eyes, a gesture that didn't go unnoticed by George.

'Yes, that's the one,' George said, stepping in. 'How familiar are you with it?'

'Considering it's not my discipline, there's not much I don't know. My wife's obsessed with it. It seems to occupy her every thought.'

There was a hint of concern in the man's voice. How deep did Rathbone's obsession with the theory go?

'Why do you believe your wife's so caught up in Hargrove's theory?' Whitney asked.

'In all honesty, I think, in part, it's because she's working on something similar, and she believes that his theory is no better than hers but he's getting all the attention,' Barton explained.

'Is that justified?' George asked.

'It's not my field, so it would be remiss of me to make a judgement.'

'Even though you told us that there wasn't much you don't know about it?'

He sucked in a breath. 'I'm only aware of it from my wife's perspective – my previous comment was more a figure of speech.'

'I haven't come across your wife's research. Where has it been submitted?' George asked.

'She hasn't yet. She's a perfectionist and keeps rewriting.' He gave a shrug.

'In which case, how can she be frustrated at the acclaim Hargrove received if her work isn't yet in the public domain?' George asked, feeling bewildered.

'My sentiments exactly.'

'Can I confirm with you that your wife is diabetic?' Whitney asked, her question direct and to the point. The man's expression changed to one of surprise.

'Yes, why?' he asked, clearly puzzled by the line of questioning. 'Is she okay?'

'As we've already mentioned, we believe so. But we do know that she had one of her hypos whilst she was there. It happened on Monday. She was fine after that,' Whitney said.

'Oh.' Barton nodded. 'It was probably because she forgot to

eat. It happens when she gets engrossed in whatever it is she's doing. Then we have trouble,' he explained.

'Does your wife have her own study?' Whitney asked.

'Yes.'

'We'd like to take a look at it.'

'Why?' He frowned.

Whitney leant in slightly, indicating the seriousness of their enquiry. 'I'm sorry to have to tell you this, Mr Barton, but we suspect your wife's involved in the suspicious deaths of three people at the conference.'

'Miranda? No way. That's ridiculous.' The man's genuine shock and disbelief were clear. 'Who died?'

'Professor Jonathan Hargrove, Dr Valerie Jenkins, and Dr Toby Merchant, who was Hargrove's research assistant. Are you familiar with these names?' Whitney asked.

The man's face paled. Was he now realising the gravity of the situation?

'Certainly the first two,' he said, his voice quivering slightly, as if he was struggling to comprehend the situation. 'And you think that Miranda had something to do with it?'

'That's what we need to question her about.'

'How did they die?'

'It's not public knowledge at the moment, but it was due to an overdose of insulin,' George said, watching the man closely.

'And you think...' The man leant forwards on his chair, his hands trembling on his knees. 'Oh my God. I know she's obsessed, but never would I have thought...' A flicker of understanding flashed across the man's face, his eyes widening with the shock of realisation.

'Mr Barton, please may we look at Miranda's study?' Whitney asked, her voice gentle yet insistent.

'Yes, of course,' he said, standing up and walking as if on autopilot. 'It's this way.' They followed him out of the room, down the corridor, and into another room.

'Miranda's study is here. Mine's upstairs.'

They walked in, and George's eyes were immediately drawn to a corkboard that covered the width of the wall beside the window. It was filled with pictures of serial killers, and also pictures of Rathbone with Hargrove, Jenkins, and also McDonnell.

'Didn't you think that this was a bit obsessive?' George asked Barton, pointing at the board.

'Well, she was engrossed in her work and also her view of the theory,' he replied, trying to justify what they were seeing.

George wasn't convinced. The intensity of Rathbone's obsession seemed to go beyond professional interest.

'Why do you think that she was so angry with these people?' Whitney asked.

'My wife is very conscientious in her work. She's very clever, but not one for putting herself forward, and often gets overlooked because of this introversion. That's all I can think of. She wants the limelight, but she's scared to make the initial step. But then she leaves herself open to other people stealing her thunder,' he explained.

George pondered over the man's words, considering how Rathbone's professional frustrations might have driven her to extreme actions. The pieces of the puzzle were slowly coming together, painting a troubling picture.

His phone pinged, indicating a text had arrived. He pulled it out of his pocket. 'It's from Miranda,' he said, his voice reflecting a mix of surprise and concern.

'What does she say?' Whitney asked.

'There's a family crisis. She's had a call from her aunt and she doesn't know when she'll be back.' He appeared genuinely perplexed.

'Do you know this aunt?'

'Not really. Her family live in Scotland.'

'And you've never met them?' Whitney asked.

Barton shook his head, his eyes glazing over like his mind was elsewhere. 'No – she likes to keep that part of her life totally separate.'

'Weren't you even curious?' Whitney asked.

'Initially, but Miranda refused to discuss them. All I know is that there's something murky about her past, but I've never found out what.' The man's voice trailed off, hinting at unresolved mysteries in their personal life.

There was more to Miranda's story than met the eye.

'She doesn't have a Scottish accent, though.'

'When she's angry it's possible to discern, other than that no. She trained it out of herself because it helped her to fit in better... at least that's what she told me... but now... I don't know what to think.' He gave a sigh.

'Do you think she might be going to Scotland?' Whitney pushed.

'According to this text, yes,' he replied, not sounding totally convinced.

The man was clearly grappling with the reality of the situation, his mind trying to piece together the fragmented information.

'Do you have any idea to which part of Scotland she might be heading?' George asked.

'I believe Glasgow is where her family live. If that's the truth. But I couldn't tell you exactly where in the area.'

'Right, if your wife does return, or contact you again, you must let us know immediately. We don't expect you to warn her that we are looking for her, either,' Whitney instructed firmly.

'But—'

'No *but*s. It's for her own good,' Whitney added, leaving no room for negotiation.

'Okay,' he agreed, albeit reluctantly.

They left the house and walked back to the car. A sense of unease about the whole situation coursed through George.

'Do you believe that he knows nothing?' Whitney asked once they were in the car.

'Judging by his body language, yes. He was genuinely stunned when we told him about the murders. Also, I believe that he doesn't know where in Scotland she's intending on going.'

'We need to find out if she really is driving there, because it's a long way.'

'She could have abandoned her car and be catching the train to stop us from tracing her car,' George speculated, her thoughts racing with possible scenarios.

'Good point,' Whitney acknowledged, pulling out her phone, and hit a number on speed dial. 'Ellie, it's me. Find out from DVLA what car Rathbone drives and do an ANPR search on her numberplate. It's my guess that she's heading towards Lenchester train station. We can't let her get away.'

TWENTY-EIGHT

Friday

Whitney's phone rang after they'd barely been driving for ten minutes. She put it on speaker. 'Hi, Ellie. What have you got for us?'

'You were right, guv. Rathbone's car's been spotted heading towards Lenchester train station.'

Whitney's insides clenched. The woman was in reach and there was no way she was going to escape.

'That's great, thanks. We'll head straight there. Arrange for the others to meet us but instruct them to stay in their cars and out of sight. If Rathbone's there, we don't want to alert her.'

'Yes, guv.'

Whitney ended the call with a decisive tap on her phone.

'How quickly can we get to the station?' she asked, turning to George.

'Twenty-five minutes, providing the lights are with us,' George replied, her voice steady.

'Good. I'm going to google the times of trains to Glasgow.' Whitney's fingers moved swiftly over the keys. 'Okay, there's one in an hour. So let's assume she's aiming to be on it. Put your foot down, George. This time I really mean it.'

George did as instructed and they arrived at their destination within twenty minutes.

They strode straight to the station office and up to the woman behind the desk.

'DCI Walker from Lenchester CID. I need to check CCTV footage. We're looking for someone who might've bought a ticket to Glasgow within the last half an hour.' Whitney held out her warrant card for the woman to see.

'I'll have to call the manager,' the woman behind the desk said, getting up and poking her head around the open door.

Whitney gave an exasperated sigh. It was like déjà vu with the conference centre and the person on duty having to get permission from their boss.

A few seconds later, a man walked out. 'I'm the station manager. How can I help you?' he asked.

'We need to see your CCTV footage. We believe a woman who's a person of interest in a murder investigation has bought a ticket to Glasgow. She's not to get on the train,' Whitney explained, urgently.

'Okay, come on through,' he said. 'We've got a screen in my office.' Whitney followed, hoping they weren't too late to catch Rathbone.

They entered the room, and on the wall was a big screen showing about twenty smaller areas. He pointed to them. 'These are all the places where we have cameras,' he explained. 'I'll bring up a bigger picture of the ticket office.'

'Thanks. We're looking at about half an hour ago, but run the footage from forty minutes just in case,' Whitney said. 'And play at double time, so we can be quick.' She leant forward, her eyes intently focused on the screen.

Whitney stared at the enlarged screen showing people buying tickets. George, next to her, did the same.

'There she is,' George announced after a couple of minutes. Whitney's eyes locked on to the figure on the screen. 'But she's not alone. That looks like Emily Davies.'

'Yes, it is,' Whitney confirmed. 'Why would Emily be with Rathbone, especially under these circumstances?'

'She doesn't appear happy to be there,' George observed.

'You're right,' Whitney agreed, her voice laced with concern. 'Rathbone might be forcing her. Can we check whether she bought tickets to Scotland?'

'Yes, give me a second,' the manager said, turning to the computer on his screen. 'Yes, two tickets for the next train to Glasgow, which leaves in thirty minutes.'

'We might have to delay it,' Whitney said, thinking ahead to their options.

'I'd rather we didn't, because if you do that, it has a domino effect on all the other trains,' the manager cautioned.

'We'll see if we can get to them first. Where did they go after buying their tickets? Can we follow them?'

'Yes,' he said, pulling up the other screens.

They followed on-screen Rathbone and Emily Davies until they reached a café and stood still.

'Emily Davies definitely appears out of sorts,' George noted, her observation echoing Whitney's earlier thoughts.

'You're not wrong,' Whitney added, her concern growing.

'Do you think Rathbone has kidnapped her?'

'I'm not sure, but I've got Emily Davies' number. I'll try it.' Whitney quickly called but it went through to voicemail. Whitney didn't leave a message, not wanting to alert Rathbone that she was monitoring Emily.

'Look, they've now gone into the café,' the manager pointed out. 'This is real time.'

'Thanks. Is that the only entrance?'

'No. There's another one coming from Platform Two.'

'Okay, thanks. That's good to know. Hopefully, we won't

need to hold up the train, but you need to be prepared for that to happen. It's not to leave until I've given you permission,' Whitney instructed, leaving no room for misunderstanding.

'All right,' he agreed, seeming to understand the gravity of the situation.

They stepped outside, and Whitney immediately called Brian. 'Where are you?' she asked, scanning the area as she spoke.

'In the car park,' came the reply.

'Leave the cars and meet me outside the ticket office. Rathbone is in the station café with Emily Davies, who doesn't appear to be there willingly.'

Whitney could see the café entrance from where they were standing. Hopefully it wasn't too busy and they could ensure Rathbone didn't escape.

'What's the plan?' George enquired, her expression serious and focused.

'When the others arrive, they can stay outside whilst we attempt to persuade Rathbone to come with us. If she tries to do a runner, we'll be able to stop her.' A surge of determination flooded through Whitney, her thoughts racing as she anticipated any unforeseen complications.

'It's worth a try,' George acknowledged.

Frank, Doug, Meena, and Brian all turned up within a minute.

'Okay, stay here. Make sure both entrances to the café are covered. George and I will try to persuade Rathbone to come with us, and Emily Davies... We'll decide about her when we're there. We don't know if Rathbone's armed, but she certainly appears to be holding Davies against her will.' Whitney looked at each member of the team, ensuring they all understood the plan. 'Don't do anything stupid, and follow my lead.'

'Yes, guv, we know the drill,' Frank responded.

'Good.' Whitney approached the café with George right

beside her. They headed to the back where Emily and Rathbone were sitting. Rathbone didn't notice them immediately, but Emily did, and her shocked and terrified expression was unmistakable.

'Miranda,' Whitney called out, her voice calm so as not to alert other people in the café. The woman turned and looked at her. 'You're to come with us. We know what's happened, and I want you down at the station so we can talk about it.'

'I'm not going anywhere. Go away.' Rathbone's voice was defiant, her posture rigid.

'Let's not make a scene here, Miranda. You and Emily are to leave the café with us.' Whitney's approach was diplomatic but firm, her eyes locked on Rathbone.

'Go away, or she gets it.' Rathbone nodded at Emily.

'She's just pulled a syringe out of her pocket. It's in her right hand.' George's voice cut through the tension.

'Yes, well spotted, Dr Cavendish,' Rathbone said sarcastically, her attention shifting between Whitney and George. 'And it's full of insulin. So you're going to step to the side while Emily and I leave to catch the train.'

'The train to Glasgow?' Whitney interjected, her voice steady despite the escalating situation.

'How do you know that?' Rathbone said, her mouth open.

'Because we do. We were with your husband when you messaged him.' Whitney's manner was matter-of-fact, revealing their upper hand in the situation.

'Damn, I knew I shouldn't have done that. Stupid of me. But we're still getting on the train, and you're going to let us, because otherwise, Emily's going to die. And believe me, you won't be able to stop it. There's enough insulin in this syringe for her to be gone within thirty seconds.' Rathbone's threat was clear.

'Okay, okay,' Whitney said, raising her hands in a calming gesture. 'You can go.'

'You and Dr Cavendish can walk ahead of us, and if you have any officers outside, you tell them to leave us alone.'

Whitney's eyes scanned for an opening to de-escalate the situation without harm. But there was nothing. Not yet.

Whitney and George swiftly headed out, their steps measured and deliberate. Whitney kept glancing over her shoulder, eyeing Rathbone, who was holding Emily very close to her. As Rathbone walked out of the café door onto the platform, Whitney nodded to her two officers, so they knew to let the women through.

'Okay, everyone back,' Rathbone commanded authoritatively, her grip on Emily tightening.

If necessary, Whitney would let them get on the train, if that's what it took to prevent another person from dying; they would just get it stopped further down the line. Brian and Meena stood back whilst Rathbone and Emily walked past, and Whitney and George discreetly followed a couple of yards behind.

As they were walking, Emily suddenly pulled herself out of Rathbone's grasp and pushed her hard, knocking the woman to the ground. Whitney's reflexes kicked in instantly. She and George raced over. Whitney swiftly grabbed hold of Rathbone's arm, her fingers wrapping tightly around the wrist. She twisted it until Rathbone dropped the syringe, her face contorted with pain and surprise.

'Get off!' Rathbone shouted, struggling under Whitney's firm grip.

Whitney, with a surge of adrenaline, dragged Rathbone to her feet and swiftly turned her around. 'Miranda Rathbone, I'm arresting you on suspicion of the murders of Jonathan Hargrove, Valerie Jenkins, and Toby Merchant. Also for the kidnapping of Emily Davies.' Whitney's voice was steady, her training taking over as she recited the rights. 'You do not have to say anything, but it may harm your defence if you do not mention something which you later rely on in court. Anything you do say may be given in evidence. Do you understand?'

'Whatever,' Rathbone said as Whitney handcuffed her.

Whitney glanced at George, who was checking on Emily Davies, ensuring she was safe and unharmed.

Rathbone, now secured, glared defiantly, but the resignation in her eyes was evident. A wave of relief washed over Whitney. They'd prevented another tragedy. As Rathbone was led away, the platform buzzed with the activity of officers and onlookers, but Whitney's focus was singular: ensuring Rathbone faced justice for her actions.

TWENTY-NINE

Friday

'Guv,' Brian called out when George and Whitney walked into the incident room, having made a detour to the station café for a coffee because it had been hours since Whitney had had one. She'd insisted that if they didn't stop, she wouldn't be responsible for her actions. Although that might have been a slight exaggeration, George was fully aware of what Whitney was like if she didn't get her regular caffeine fix. So, she was happy to go along with it.

'What is it, Brian?' Whitney said, indicating she was ready to get back to business.

'It turns out that Rathbone's solicitor has another appointment and can't make it over today. He'll be here first thing tomorrow morning,' the detective sergeant informed them.

Whitney's jaw tightened – a sure sign of her frustration at the delay.

'Does Rathbone know about this?' Whitney asked with a sigh.

'Yes, she's prepared to wait. She's refusing to talk without her solicitor present. Her husband's been in touch, wanting to know what's happening.'

'What did you tell him?' Whitney enquired.

'That his wife's in custody and that he can't see her.'

'Okay, that's fine. If we have to wait to speak to Rathbone, we might as well talk to Emily Davies. Where is she?'

'She's in one of the nicer interview rooms with a cup of tea,' Brian answered.

'Has she been checked over by a medical examiner?' Outwardly Emily Davies had appeared okay, but Whitney wanted to be sure.

'Yes, the doctor's been, and she doesn't need to go to the hospital. She's not injured.'

'Excellent,' Whitney said, her shoulders relaxing. 'Okay. Right, George and I are going to have a chat with Emily. We'll see what else we can glean so that we're fully informed for Rathbone's interview tomorrow. The rest of you, continue looking into all the victims and Rathbone. I want us to make sure there's nothing that's going to jump out at us later,' Whitney finished speaking, her eyes moving over the team, ensuring they'd grasped the significance of being meticulous in their investigation.

'Yes, guv,' they all responded in unison.

'And what about a celebration now the case is over, guv? Shall we go out for a drink after work?' Frank called out with his usual enthusiasm, as they went to leave the incident room.

Whitney stopped walking and turned back to face the team. 'We'll wait until after Rathbone's interview tomorrow and it's all sorted. Then, and only then, can we go out to celebrate.'

'Oh, okay,' Frank said, a hint of disappointment in his voice. 'I was hoping we could go out tonight. The wife's sister's coming round *again*. Seriously, I don't know why she doesn't just move in she's there so often... and you know what her being there means: chat, chat, chat, chat, chat. I was hoping for a bit of overtime to get some peace and quiet.'

'You go home and enjoy yourself,' Doug said, a smirk on his face. 'You know you like it, really.'

'How the hell do you know?' Frank retorted, his brows raised in mock indignation.

'Because I know what you're like. You can chat with the best of them,' Doug said, causing a wave of chuckles to ripple through the room.

'Okay, okay,' Whitney intervened, bringing the focus back to the task at hand. 'George and I are off.'

George smiled to herself as they left. Frank and Doug's little spats were both legendary and amusing, even though the men were very fond of each other. George often mused over their dynamic, appreciating the way they injected lighter moments into the seriousness of their work.

They headed down the corridor in the direction of the stairs to take them down to the interview room.

'Do you wish me to observe from another room, or be part of the interview?' George asked.

'You can be with me. Do you think that Emily was originally part of the scheme but then Rathbone double-crossed her?' Whitney replied, turning to her friend, frowning.

It was a plausible theory, and George knew they needed to explore all angles. 'It's something we can put to her, but from when we questioned her yesterday, none of her body language alerted me. I believe that she was – or at least genuinely thought she was – in a relationship with Rathbone, but that's all,' George said, her analytical mind weighing the possibilities.

When they entered the interview room, Emily glanced up from the easy chair she was sitting in. Her face was pale and drawn. She appeared in shock. George glanced at the coffee table where there was an untouched mug of tea.

'You're not having anything to drink?' Whitney asked, appearing to note Emily's apparent distress.

'No, I don't feel like it,' Emily said, her voice barely above a whisper.

They sat down opposite her.

'How are you feeling?' George asked, gently, trying to make Emily feel at ease.

'Stupid,' she muttered.

'What do you mean?' Whitney asked, leaning in slightly, showing her engagement with Emily's story.

'This whole thing. The relationship, everything. I thought Miranda really liked me, but it was all a lie.' Emily's voice was tinged with sadness and betrayal.

'What do you mean?' Whitney enquired further, her focus on understanding the situation fully.

'Because she told me.'

'Why don't you go through everything that happened today?' Whitney suggested, kindly. 'Take it slowly, bit by bit.'

Emily nodded and drew in a sharp breath. 'Because you'd already spoken to Miranda, she told me that she was allowed to leave, and also that I was allowed to go with her.'

'But you were in the conference room when we'd divided everyone into groups,' Whitney said, sounding puzzled.

'Yes. Miranda was there, too. Once you'd made the announcement and had taken some of the others with you for their interview, she came over to me.'

'And you believed that it was okay for you to go, even after DCI Walker had specifically said that no one should?' George asked, her brows furrowed in confusion.

'Well, yes, because you'd already interviewed both of us. I said to Miranda that I wanted to check, but she promised that there was no need. She said she'd take me to the station, so I could catch the train home.'

'How did you manage to get past the security on the door?' Whitney asked.

'The conference centre security guard was standing outside, and when we left the building, Miranda said you'd given us permission to leave because we had an appointment. The security guy believed her and let us go.'

Whitney gave a frustrated sigh. 'I see,' she said through clenched teeth.

'Okay, so you got into her car, and then what happened?' George asked, taking over from Whitney whilst piecing together the sequence of events.

'Miranda started questioning me about what I told you about her, and I said nothing. Then she just laughed and said, "That's okay, then." She told me that we were going away to Scotland. When I told her that I didn't want to go, she said it wasn't up for negotiation because she wasn't going to leave any loose ends.'

'Did you understand what she meant at that time?' Whitney asked.

'Not really. But she was in a strange mood and I didn't want to annoy her, so I just went along with it. I thought that once we got to the station, I could refuse to go with her and get on a train home.'

'When you were at the station and Miranda bought the ticket, it looked like she was coercing you. She'd got hold of your arm. Is that correct?' George asked, trying to clarify the details.

'Yes, because I told her not to get me a ticket because I wasn't going with her. She said that I was and that if I tried to get away, she'd do to me what she did to Hargrove, Jenkins, and Merchant. And then I realised...'

'What did you realise?' Whitney asked.

'That she'd killed them and she was going to kill me.'

'Did she tell you how she'd do that?' Whitney asked gravely.

'Yes, she said she'd got a syringe in her pocket that was full of insulin, and if I tried to move, she'd stab me with it. She said I'd be dead straight away.'

'And you believed her?' Whitney asked, her concern evident.

'Of course I believed her. I knew that the other three were dead. I feel like such an idiot because it showed that she'd never felt anything for me. She used me to find out about the conference.'

'Did Miranda know that we were on to her when she left a message for her husband, telling him where you were going?' Whitney asked.

'No. She only messaged him so that he didn't worry about her and alert the police. But when he messaged her back, telling her to come home, she became suspicious.'

'Why? Did he say that we were looking for her?' Whitney asked moving closer.

'No, but she somehow realised that it must be because you were looking for her. I think it was because normally he wouldn't ask her not to go somewhere.'

'Then what happened?'

'We went to the café and a little bit later, you came into the restaurant. The rest you know.'

Emily's recounting of the events filled in many gaps for George. Emily's vulnerability and Rathbone's manipulation were clear.

'Going back to when you first met, you said you went to one of her lectures and then you got together. Was that before or after you'd decided to go to the conference as an organiser?' George asked.

'Before. Miranda suggested I should attend with her,' Emily replied, her voice showing a hint of realisation as she recounted the events. George could see the dawning awareness in Emily's eyes, the understanding that her involvement had been orchestrated from the start. 'She said that the conference was coming up and it would be really good for me because of the papers being presented and the panels. I couldn't afford to go and so she suggested that I applied for a job as an organiser. She gave me the contact details of the person in charge. Miranda said they're always looking for people to help, and if I offered my services, especially because of what I've studied, then I would likely be able to get a job helping. There's no payment, but it meant I could attend all the presentations.'

'It's a most prestigious conference,' George agreed, her voice empathetic, understanding how enticing the opportunity must have been for Emily.

'Yes, it is,' Emily continued. 'And that's what happened. Now I know she was just using me.'

'Once you'd applied and been accepted, did your relationship develop?' George asked, seeking clarification on how deep it had gone.

'Yes, we'd see each other when we could.'

'When we've finished interviewing you, is there anyone you can be with?' Whitney asked.

'I'm going to stay with my parents for a few days, if that's okay,' Emily said, her voice small, making her look much younger than her years.

'Where do they live?'

'Guildford. My dad's on his way to collect me.'

'Okay, as long as we've got your details. We do need to take a formal statement from you,' Whitney said.

'Does it have to be today?' Emily asked, looking exhausted and staring directly at Whitney.

'No. We'll contact you next week and arrange a time for you to come in,' Whitney reassured her.

'Okay, thank you,' Emily said, her relief evident.

'You can stay here until your father arrives.'

'Thank you.' Emily sank back in her chair, her face drawn.

Whitney and George left the room, their steps echoing softly.

'Okay, that's as much as we can do today. I'm going to visit Mum and take Rob, Tiffany, and Ava. What do you have planned?' Whitney asked.

'More wedding stuff.' George grimaced. 'Although I believe most of it is done, other than a few small bits and pieces. After that, we thought we'd have a quiet night in, which will be most welcome.'

'Enjoy. Can you come in tomorrow when we interview Rathbone?'

'You couldn't keep me away,' George insisted.

THIRTY

Friday

'Okay, everyone,' Whitney said as she got out of the car with Rob, Tiffany and Ava. 'I want you to remember that Mum – Granny – might not be like she normally is.'

'What do you mean, Whitney?' Rob asked, his nose wrinkled in confusion. 'You told me that she was getting better.'

'Yes, she is, Rob, but sometimes she goes into a bit of a dream and forgets where she is. You know that. You've seen it happen before.' Whitney's voice was soft yet firm, trying to prepare them for the potential reality inside.

'Come... come...' Ava said, pulling Tiffany's hand.

'Okay, we're going to see Granny.'

'Now, don't get too excited, because there are a lot of people in there. Remember.' Whitney glanced down at Ava, who grinned in return. She was such an adorable little girl. Even if Whitney was biased.

'Yes, Mum,' Tiffany said, as if she was humouring Whitney.

'Hopefully she'll be fine, I just want to prepare you.'

'It's okay, Mum. We understand, don't we, Uncle Rob?' Tiffany said, looking up at Rob.

'Yes, we do,' Rob replied, but Whitney wasn't totally convinced.

'Granny shall be very surprised to see us all. But if it gets too much for her, we'll have to leave. I don't want any complaints if I suggest it.' Whitney took a deep breath as they walked towards the entrance to the care home.

Angela was sitting behind the reception desk and she gave a broad smile as they approached.

'How's she doing?' Whitney asked, unable to hide her concern.

'A lot better, Whitney. A lot better. Honestly, we were surprised at how quickly she recovered. She still drifts in and out as she was before, but there's very little difference between how she was before the fall and after.' Angela's words were reassuring, and Whitney felt a sense of relief.

'Thank goodness for that. Where is she?'

'In the day room. We told her that you were going to visit because we didn't want to give her too much of a shock if you all turned up unexpectedly to see her.'

'Thanks so much.' Whitney smiled, her heart lightening with the news of her mum's improvement. 'Come on, you lot, let's go,' Whitney said, her voice tinged with a mix of anticipation and concern.

They walked down into the day room, which had seen better days decor-wise, but it was comfortable, and her mum loved it. Whitney noted the familiar surroundings, feeling a sense of nostalgia.

Her mum was sitting in a chair, staring at the television. Ava pulled out of Tiffany's hand and ran over to her. Whitney's mum's eyes lit up when she saw her great-granddaughter.

Whitney exchanged a glance with Tiffany, communicating

her relief and happiness at this small but significant moment. It was such a difference between when she'd seen her a few days ago. She was like a different person.

'Hi, Mum,' Whitney said as they got there, her voice warm and gentle.

'Hello, Granny,' Tiffany added, giving her grandmother a kiss on the cheek.

'Hello, Mum,' Rob chimed in, his voice filled with a mixture of excitement and caution.

'What are you all doing here?' her mother asked, a hint of surprise in her voice.

'Angela said they told you we were popping in to see you.'

'Did they?' her mother replied, a bit confused, which was not uncommon given her condition.

'Well, it's good to see you looking better because the last time I saw you, you weren't at all well,' Whitney said.

'When was that?' her mother asked, genuinely puzzled.

'I came to see you after you had the fall. Remember?'

'Did I? Oh, well, that's why I've got bruises on my legs, then. I didn't know. Nobody told me.' Her mother sounded confused.

'I think they probably did, Mum, but you've forgotten. Let's all sit down. We're not going to stay long in case you get tired.'

'You stay as long as you like,' her mother responded, clearly warming up to the company. 'Apart from when my programme starts. Then you'll have to go,' she added.

'We understand,' Whitney replied, smiling softly.

The visit was bittersweet, a reminder of the changes in her mother's condition, but Whitney was grateful for these moments of clarity and connection.

'So, what has my big boy been doing?' Whitney's mum asked, turning her attention to Rob.

Whitney watched, a smile playing on her lips as she observed the interaction between her brother and mother.

'I baked you a cake, Mum, but I had to give some of it to Whitney because it wouldn't have lasted when you were sick,' Rob proudly stated, his eyes lighting up with the mention of his culinary efforts.

'Oh, that sounds lovely. What sort was it?' her mum enquired, her eyes brightening with mischief.

'Your favourite – chocolate cake,' Rob replied, his chest puffing out with pride.

'Then it must have tasted delicious.'

'I'll make another one for you again soon.'

'I'll look forward to that, thank you.' Her mother's words were warm and appreciative. 'And Tiffany, what are you up to?' she asked, shifting her focus.

'I'm going back to uni to finish off my degree,' Tiffany replied, her voice carrying a mix of excitement and nervousness.

'Oh, that's good. Such a clever girl, isn't she, Whitney?' Her mum turned to Whitney, seeking confirmation.

'Yes.' Whitney nodded, her heart swelling with pride at her daughter's achievements.

'She must be the cleverest person in the whole family.'

'Mum's very clever too,' Tiffany added.

'Oh, but you're very, *very* clever. You're going to university. And what subject are you going to study?' her mother asked.

'Engineering. Do you remember that I started a few years ago, and then dropped out because I went to Australia?' Tiffany explained, recounting her academic journey.

'Australia, that must have been fantastic,' Whitney's mother commented with a mix of awe and nostalgia.

'It was lovely, Granny. But very hot.'

'And now you're back home?' Whitney's mum continued, trying to piece together Tiffany's story.

'I've been home for over two years, Granny.' Tiffany's voice trailed off.

'Ah, yes, so you have. I remember. Because of lovely Ava.

How old are you now?' Her attention turned to her great-granddaughter.

'She's two,' Tiffany said, her voice filled with affection. 'And she's into everything.'

'Sounds just like your mum. Whitney was like that, drove us all mad, she did. Question after question. That's why her dad renamed her *Why-tney*,' her mother reminisced, a hint of humour in her voice.

'Yes, I think we all know that story, Mum,' Whitney said, having heard it a million times. She felt a mix of nostalgia and amusement at the familiar anecdote, grateful for these moments of lucidity and shared memories with her mother.

'So, are you busy at work, Whitney?' her mum asked.

'I'm afraid I am, Mum... as usual.'

'Not more people dying?'

'You know what it's like around here. Never a moment's peace.' Whitney's voice was light, trying to keep the conversation easy.

'I'm glad you came to see me, anyway.' Her mum's words were genuine, and Whitney felt a pang of guilt for not having the time to visit more regularly.

'I'm sorry it can't be more often,' Whitney said.

'And Rob, what are you up to now?' Her mum turned back to Rob.

'I'm in charge of setting the table where I live.' Rob's chest puffed out again with pride at his accomplishment.

'That's excellent. We always knew you were good at organising things and keeping everything in order.' Her mum's praise warmed Whitney's heart, happy to see her brother being acknowledged. 'Right now, I think my programme's about to start soon,' her mother remarked, glancing at the television.

'Okay, Mum,' Whitney said, sensing the need not to disrupt her mum's routine.

'You can sit with me and watch if you like.' The invitation

was genuine, and Whitney appreciated the gesture. 'Ava, come and sit on your great-granny's lap.'

Whitney exchanged a glance with Tiffany. It was interesting how one minute her mum was a bit vague and then the next, she knew that Ava was her great-granddaughter. Ava obliged, ran over, and Whitney's mum lifted her up and sat her on her lap. 'I want everyone to be quiet. A very important someone is about to be murdered.'

Whitney was immediately concerned about what exactly they were going to be watching. 'I'm not sure that this will be suitable for Ava, Mum.'

'Don't be silly, it's a soap. It's not real,' her mother responded, dismissing Whitney's concern.

'Still, I don't think it's appropriate,' Whitney reiterated, knowing her mother's strong-willed nature and trying to reason with her.

'Oh.' Her mum's face fell.

'I tell you what, you watch, and we'll go and come back another time.'

'And bring your chocolate cake with you.'

'Definitely,' Whitney said.

'I hope I'll like it. I've never had chocolate cake before,' she said, a dreamy expression on her face.

Whitney's heart dropped. Her mum was definitely drifting off again.

'You have, Mum,' Whitney assured her.

'Goodbye.' Her mum dismissed them with a wave of her hand.

Whitney glanced at Tiffany. It was time to leave.

Once outside, Whitney took a deep breath, feeling the weight of the visit. 'It's the dementia,' Whitney said to Rob and Tiffany, wanting to explain even though they realised. 'One minute she's fine, the next she's somewhere else. But she's a lot better than she was a few days ago. Come on, we'll stop off at the burger place before we go home.'

'Hurray. My favourite,' Rob said. 'Can I have a double cheeseburger and a chocolate milkshake?'

'Of course you can.' Whitney led them back to the car, her mind still on her mum, but looking forward to spending some relaxed time with her family.

THIRTY-ONE

Saturday

Whitney walked into the incident room early, her steps steady and determined. Already, the team were seated at their desks, engrossed in their work. 'Morning, everyone,' Whitney greeted, as she surveyed the room. 'I want as much as possible on Rathbone before the interview, which is due to take place at nine o'clock. Do we have anything yet?'

'Actually, guv, I do. I came across it last night, but wanted to delve into it further before sharing. It's about Rathbone's background,' Ellie said.

Whitney took a few steps towards the officer, her interest piqued. 'What is it?'

'Rathbone isn't her real surname. Her original name was Eltham,' Ellie revealed.

The woman had changed her identity.

Why? And why did Whitney have the feeling that she'd heard the name before?

'That rings a bell,' Frank said, joining the conversation.

'Yes, for me, too,' Doug added.

'I thought the same,' Whitney agreed. 'But why?'

'If I give you the full name of her father, that might help,' Ellie suggested, grinning.

Whitney noted the lightness in her officer's voice. Was she feeling a little better after the break-up?

'Well, come on then, Ellie,' Whitney urged. 'Don't keep us all hanging on.'

'Her father's name was Kelvin Eltham,' Ellie said.

'From Dumfries, in Scotland?' Brian called out, joining in.

A jolt of recognition washed over Whitney. 'I remember. He was convicted of killing seven sex workers in the 1980s.'

'Yes, that's it. It was in all the media at the time,' Ellie said.

'So, what you're saying is that our serial killer is herself the daughter of a serial killer?' Whitney clarified, her mind racing with the implications of this revelation.

'Exactly that,' Ellie confirmed.

The door opened and George walked in.

'Dr C, you'll never guess what we've found out,' Frank called out.

Whitney let out a laugh, appreciating the light-hearted moment amidst the tension.

George frowned, clearly puzzled. 'I don't enjoy guessing games.'

'We'll put you out of your misery, then,' Whitney said. 'We've discovered that Rathbone changed her name by deed poll. I believe that's correct. Ellie?'

'Yes, guv,' Ellie confirmed. 'Her name used to be Melody Eltham, daughter of Kelvin Eltham.'

'A serial killer of sex workers, from Dumfries. I've read several papers on him,' George said. 'My goodness. And Miranda Rathbone is his daughter?'

'Yes, that's correct. Which is something that we'll be questioning her on during the interview.'

'Her response to that will be fascinating,' George said. 'It could make a big difference to understanding her motivation.'

Whitney stood back, her mind already formulating questions for Rathbone. 'I agree. Is there anything else we've discovered about the woman?'

'I've been looking into her social media accounts,' Meena said. 'Although she does have them, she rarely posts. I would guess that she's a very private person.'

'It would back up what her husband told us, that she's an introvert,' Whitney explained.

'She doesn't appear to participate in research conferences or give presentations,' Ellie added from her desk. 'She lectures but doesn't publish papers.'

'That's probably because she's so engrossed in her own theory that she doesn't have time for much else,' George interjected. 'Her husband also mentioned that she's a perfectionist and continually rewrites. I'm surprised her university has allowed her not to publish regularly. Funding is dependent on research outputs. We'd need to see her contract of employment to understand how she got away with that exactly. Although I suspect it's not an important factor in the investigation.'

Whitney appreciated George's input, not only because of her analytical skills and attention to detail, but her experience in an educational environment. 'When we spoke to her husband, he said that research into serial killers is her life's work, and she didn't want Hargrove and the rest of them stealing her thunder. We'll base our interview on this.'

'I don't get it. How can she be an introvert if she's a lecturer?' Frank questioned.

Whitney turned to George, nodding for her input.

'It's more common than you think, Frank. When Rathbone is lecturing, she'll hide behind her subject matter. She's not putting herself on display. When she's at the podium, all the students are witnessing is her understanding of the subject matter. I would be very surprised if she gives away anything about herself, such as personal anecdotes, like some lecturers do.'

'I didn't realise that,' Frank admitted, shaking his head. 'I just thought anyone who taught was an outgoing show-off.'

'If that were true, you'd make an amazing teacher, then.' Doug smirked.

'Yeah, well, you would say that. What about you? You're—'

The phone rang on the desk, putting a halt to the conversation.

'DCI Walker, good morning,' Whitney said, her voice professional and crisp.

'Rathbone's solicitor has arrived,' the desk sergeant said.

Whitney glanced at her watch. 'They're early. That must be a first.'

'Yes. It's because they have another appointment. Can you bring the interview forward?'

'I don't see why not. We'll be down shortly,' Whitney responded, replacing the phone. 'Rathbone's solicitor's here. George, you can watch. Brian, come with me. The rest of you, more digging, in case you find anything else. And I'd like to know more about Rathbone's father.'

On the way down to the interview, George turned to Whitney. 'We'll need to tread very carefully on this one, bearing in mind what we know about her and how introverted and obsessive she is. She's just as likely to clam up and tell you nothing.'

'How do you suggest we get it out of her, then?' Whitney asked, open to George's insight.

'First of all, I would play to her strengths. Talk about the theory, what she's done. Get her talking.'

'And then ask about the murders and motivation behind it?'

'Yes, lead on to it gradually.'

'What about mentioning her father?'

'See how that goes. I definitely wouldn't bring him up straight away,' George advised.

'Okay, thanks, George,' Whitney said, her mind already formulating the approach for the interview.

Once inside the interview room, Whitney's eyes were drawn to Rathbone's solicitor, who looked to be in her early sixties. Whitney hadn't seen her before, but surmised she probably came from the Rugby area, which was where Rathbone lived.

'Good morning,' Whitney said. She nodded to Brian, signalling him to start the recording. 'This interview will be recorded.'

'Interview on Saturday, sixteenth of March. Those present: Detective Chief Inspector Walker, Detective Sergeant Chapman...' Brian nodded towards the solicitor.

'Fiona Garland, solicitor.'

'Miranda Rathbone.'

'Right, Miranda, as you know, you're under caution, and we'd like to talk to you about the deaths of Jonathan Hargrove, Valerie Jenkins, and Toby Merchant.' Whitney's voice was firm, her eyes fixed on their suspect, who sat opposite with her arms folded. 'First of all, when we spoke to your husband, and we looked around your study, we noticed that you're researching into serial killers in much the same way as Jonathan Hargrove,' Whitney began, laying the groundwork for the interrogation.

'Who said you could go into my study?' Rathbone snapped, her eyes narrow.

Whitney's demeanour remained calm, unperturbed by the response. 'Your husband allowed us in there,' Whitney continued, unflinching.

'He shouldn't have done that. My work's private.'

'I don't know much about this area of study, so perhaps you can enlighten me. Is your theory of serial killers the same as the one Jonathan Hargrove put forward?' Whitney pressed on, steering the conversation towards Rathbone's work as George had directed.

'It's not the same as Hargrove's,' Rathbone retorted, her top lip curling.

'I see. How different is your theory?' Whitney enquired, keeping alert to Rathbone's responses in case of inconsistencies or revelations.

'Our theories are similar in many ways, but what he lacks is the deep insight. All he was interested in was pushing this theory, and as for calling it Death's Shadow... That's sensationalising and hanging on to Jung's coat-tails.' Rathbone's response was passionate, revealing her deep attachment to her work.

'Does that mean you're of a similar mind to Angus McDonnell and Valerie Jenkins, regarding what's lacking with the professor's theory?' Whitney pushed.

'Yes. We all believed that Hargrove glossed over any contentious areas.'

'And, unlike Hargrove, you've gone into sufficient depth with your theory?' Whitney's statement was a calculated move, inviting Rathbone to elaborate on her own work.

'That's correct, I have.' Rathbone's response was confident, bordering on arrogance.

'Let me get this straight. You weren't happy because Hargrove was presenting a theory that you had yourself come up with, only yours is better because you'd thought about some of the issues that he'd ignored?' Whitney's observation was sharp, aiming to get Rathbone to reveal more about her motivations.

'It's not like that,' Rathbone answered, defensively.

'What is it like, then?' Whitney asked, her curiosity evident.

'You don't understand. You're not an academic.' Rathbone's dismissal was a challenge to Whitney.

'Try me,' Whitney said, her voice calm yet assertive; she was not going to be intimidated by Rathbone's academic prowess.

'He came up with a theory. All he was interested in was the accolade achieved from proposing something so outrageous.'

'Was that why he had to die, because he was standing in the way of your work, your reputation?' Whitney's conclusion was a direct accusation; her eyes fixed on Rathbone, waiting for her reaction. She was ready to catch any slip or confession that Rathbone might inadvertently reveal.

'I'm not saying anything. You're just trying to pin the blame on me,' Rathbone retorted, her voice defensive.

'I think we're a bit past that now, don't you? We've already caught you with Emily Davies, carrying a syringe full of insulin and threatening her. That's exactly how all the victims died,' Whitney countered as she sought to break through Rathbone's defences.

'You don't understand,' Rathbone said, her eyes blazing.

'You're right, I don't. So why don't you tell me.'

'I wasn't prepared to let Hargrove continue getting it wrong. It would have set the study into serial killers back years.'

'Okay. What about Valerie Jenkins? Why did she have to go?' Whitney pushed.

'She was a potential ally of Hargrove's and could carry forward his work after he was eliminated.'

'But that's not the case. She was working with McDonnell to challenge Hargrove's theory. They intended to put forward their own view.'

'Which would have been equally incomplete,' Rathbone snapped.

'According to her,' George said in Whitney's earpiece. 'She has no proof unless she's seen their work.' Whitney nodded.

'Did you see what Jenkins and McDonnell were working on? Because how else would you be able to comment on their theory?'

Rathbone coloured and wouldn't meet Whitney's eyes. 'Not

exactly,' she muttered. 'I overheard them discussing it and knew they shouldn't be allowed to continue.'

'My view is that she was jealous. Put that to her,' George said.

'So basically, what you're saying is that Valerie Jenkins had to go because she knew everything that was wrong with Hargrove's theory and could put hers in the place of his and take the credit?' Whitney summarised. 'It's jealousy on your part.'

'No comment.'

'I think it's a bit late for that. Let's turn to Toby Merchant, Hargrove's postdoctoral research assistant. Why did he have to go? Surely you weren't jealous of him, too.'

The solicitor whispered something in Rathbone's ear.

Whitney couldn't hear what it was but could hazard a guess.

'No comment,' Rathbone said, confirming Whitney was right.

In response, Whitney gave an intentionally loud exasperated sigh. 'Okay. I'll tell you, in that case. Merchant worked on Hargrove's theory and knew enough himself to continue with the work. You couldn't bear the thought of that happening. Am I right?' Whitney locked eyes with Rathbone.

'You don't know what you're talking about. You haven't worked in the field like I have.'

Rathbone's admission was telling, and Whitney could sense her desperation to protect her work.

'Push the jealousy angle more,' George said.

Whitney nodded slightly, acknowledging George's input.

'Seems to me that you murdered those people because you saw them as a threat to your work. We already know from your husband that you're introverted. You were jealous because they had the courage to put their theories forward, weren't you?' Whitney challenged.

'It's not like that.'

'What is it like, then?'

'They don't understand. They come up with these theories, and give it that stupid Death's Shadow title. What they don't understand is the true mind of a serial killer.' Rathbone's words were defiant, her frustration evident.

'But you do, don't you?' Whitney said, her voice low and steady.

Rathbone's mouth opened. 'No comment,' she finally said, her voice low.

'Keep going, Whitney. She's about to give you something,' George encouraged in her ear.

'Suit yourself. Because I can tell you exactly why you know the mind of a serial killer. It's because you've lived with one,' Whitney continued, her eyes locked onto Rathbone as the colour slowly drained from the woman's face.

'What?' Rathbone's voice was a mix of shock and denial.

'You're Melody Eltham, the daughter of Kelvin Eltham. So, you would know better than anyone what's in the mind of a serial killer, having lived with one for so long. Right?' Whitney's question was pointed, her tone deliberate. She tilted her head slightly, aiming to unsettle Rathbone and provoke a response.

'I had no idea.' Rathbone's admission was reluctant, her voice tinged with bitterness. She fidgeted with the edge of her sleeve, avoiding eye contact. 'None of us did.'

'And you didn't suspect anything?'

'Don't you start. That's what everyone said. Our whole family life was ruined. People thought we had to know what was going on. But we didn't... and that's the truth.' Rathbone's arms were crossed and her jaw tight. The deep-seated trauma behind her words was obvious.

'Tell me about your father,' Whitney asked, sitting back in her chair, her movement measured to bring the tension down.

'He was a normal dad. No different from other dads.' Rathbone's voice was flat, her eyes distant, as if recalling memories.

'How did he act in front of your friends?' Whitney enquired softly, encouraging openness.

'I didn't have many friends.' Rathbone looked down at her hands, knotted together in her lap.

'So how do you know he was no different from other dads?' Whitney continued, her voice gentle but probing.

'I'd watch at school when parents came. My dad was just like them; he didn't seem odd or anything. But that's not unusual in serial killers.' Rathbone's words were matter-of-fact, but her shoulders slumped slightly, betraying a hint of resignation.

'She's right,' George said, nodding. 'Many of them are fully integrated in society.'

'Did he help you with your homework? Did he encourage you to do well at school?' Whitney's questions flowed smoothly, her posture open and engaged.

'Yes.' Rathbone's eyes finally met Whitney's, a flicker of something undefinable in her eyes.

'Is that why you chose to study psychology? So you could find out why your dad did what he did?' Whitney asked, her head tilted in curiosity.

'I suppose so.' Rathbone's voice was soft, almost a whisper, her eyes clouded with unspoken thoughts.

'What about the rest of your family? Do you have any siblings?' Whitney shifted in her chair, genuinely interested.

'I have an older brother.' Rathbone's eyes flickered away for a moment, a subtle hardness in her voice.

'Do you keep in contact with him?'

'No. Once I went to university, I didn't see my mum and brother again.' Rathbone's voice was steady, but her fingers twisted nervously.

'Don't you miss them?' Whitney's voice was soft, almost coaxing.

'No. I wanted to be as far away as possible from my family.' Rathbone lifted her chin defiantly.

'And so you changed your name, dropped your accent, and moved on. But what your father did never left you, did it?' Whitney pushed, trying to break through Rathbone's barriers.

'Look, I've just... I'm not saying anything else.' Rathbone's resistance was clear in her clenched fists and rigid posture, but Whitney knew they were close to unravelling her true motives.

'We understand. You lived with a serial killer. You understand what it's like, came up with a theory as a result. Because once you found out what your father had done, you could then look back for the telltale signs to prove your theory. Except, Jonathan Hargrove came up with something similar and was trying to steal your thunder. Maybe you should admit to the academic world who you are and they'll take your theory more seriously... Except, now you've become one yourself,' Whitney said, her voice calm but assertive, her hands clasped together in front of her.

'Okay. I admit it. I killed Hargrove, Jenkins and Merchant,' Rathbone said, the fight seeming to go out of her.

'I think that's enough questioning,' the solicitor interjected. 'My client needs a break.'

'Fine. We've got everything we need,' Whitney said, standing up. She and Brian left the incident room. 'Thoughts, George?' Whitney enquired as they caught up with their colleague in the corridor.

'It's as we expected.'

'Tell me... the fact that she's turned into a serial killer like her father, what does that say for this Death's Shadow theory?' Whitney asked.

'I'm not sure we can conclude anything on the strength of that. Because, as Hargrove put forward, this shadow self isn't necessarily genetic. There's nothing to prove that,' George replied.

'But we can't disprove it, either,' Whitney added, her mind grappling with the complexities of the case.

'No, but if you accept his theory that social and environmental factors can push someone into becoming a serial killer, what you're saying is that there were factors pushing her as well. So, it's not something that's in her blood,' George concluded.

'Whatever you say. My head's about to explode with all this psychological stuff. We'll go back to the office, and then later, let's grab a drink,' Whitney suggested, feeling a need to debrief and relax after the intense questioning.

She led the way, her thoughts still occupied with the case, but also looking forward to unwinding with her team.

THIRTY-TWO

Saturday

George followed Whitney into the Railway Tavern, the pub close to the station. The rest of the team were sitting at one of the large tables close to the wall. George observed the familiar, comforting setting, a place where many of their successes had been toasted.

'Right, drinks are on me,' Whitney said.

George accompanied her friend to the bar, feeling a sense of camaraderie and relief that the case had come to a close.

'Here's to the case being solved quickly,' Whitney said, once they were back with the team, holding a glass up.

'Yes, and without Dickhead's interference,' Frank added with his usual bluntness, referring to the chief superintendent.

'Now, now, Frank,' Whitney cautioned, her tone light but firm. George glanced across at Brian, who was friendly with Douglas, but he didn't seem to mind the banter.

'Well, it was touch-and-go. If we hadn't solved it so quickly, he might've made an appearance,' Frank added, acknowledging their good fortune.

'We should be thankful for small mercies, right? So, what have you got planned for the weekend, what's left of it?' Whitney asked, shifting the conversation to lighter topics.

'Oh, the wife wants me to go to the garden centre tomorrow, so I've got that to look forward to,' Frank said, sounding resigned. 'She's really getting into gardening now. I don't know why. Actually, I do. It's because she keeps watching that programme on telly and wants to totally renovate our garden, which, by the way, is no larger than a postage stamp so I'm not sure what she's thinking she can do to make it look any better.'

'George likes gardening, don't you?' Whitney asked, turning to George.

'Yes, I do,' George responded, her thoughts briefly turning to her own garden at home. She'd always found gardening to be a peaceful escape.

'Maybe you should come round to our place, Doc, and then you can help the wife out?' Frank joked.

'No, thank you, Frank. I have enough on my plate as it is,' George replied, thinking about the myriad tasks still pending for her upcoming wedding.

'Oh, you mean the wedding. Are you looking forward to it?' Frank asked.

'Frank, don't get personal,' Whitney said.

'It's fine,' George said. 'It's been time consuming and, to be honest, I'll be glad when it's over. There's an awful lot of work to do and people to consider.'

'I remember my wedding,' Frank said. 'Well, actually, I don't. I drank so much that it's all a bit of a blur. But I do remember throwing up in the bushes outside, and the wife coming out and having a go at me,' Frank recalled with a laugh, causing George to chuckle.

'Seems you started off the way you intended to go throughout the whole marriage,' Doug said, joining in the laughter.

'Well, I suppose you're right.' Frank laughed, his story bringing a moment of levity to the group.

'Ellie, what are your plans for the weekend?' Whitney asked, showing her genuine interest in her colleague's well-being.

'Not much, guv,' Ellie said.

George observed Whitney's thoughtful expression, sensing that she was considering something important.

'You know, I was thinking, now the case is over, perhaps you should have a few days off and go away somewhere. You could do with a break after everything that's been going on. You've got lots of leave owing, haven't you?' Whitney suggested.

'Yes, I have. I was thinking about going to Cornwall,' Ellie responded, her voice reflecting a mix of excitement and uncertainty.

'What's in Cornwall?' Frank asked, frowning.

'You mean *who*. It's Matt. Surely you haven't forgotten that he moved down there,' Whitney said, referring to her ex-sergeant who'd relocated to Cornwall with his young daughter to be with his parents, after his wife had tragically died.

'Oh... Yes... of course. That's a good idea,' Frank said, nodding.

'Matt's always saying I should go for a holiday.' The officer's words trailed off, her thoughts seemingly drifting to Cornwall. 'I've never been there before,' she added, a hint of excitement creeping into her voice.

'It's beautiful. You'll love it,' Whitney encouraged, her smile warm and reassuring.

'Yes, I concur. It's a lovely place. Perfect for some relaxation,' George agreed, nodding in support of the idea.

'Put in your leave request and I'll approve it straight away,' Whitney said, showing her willingness to support Ellie's decision.

'I'll have to get in touch with Matt first to see if it's okay for me to visit. I won't be able to stay with him because the house is very small, but he might be able to find somewhere close by, although he'll be working.' Ellie's contemplation was evident, her mind already planning the logistics of the trip.

'Yeah, but it will still be nice,' Whitney said. 'Have a break. You'll enjoy it. I'm sure there'll be plenty to do... have a look around... go for long walks on the beach. Penzance is meant to be absolutely lovely.'

'I'll suggest to Matt that I visit for a week.' Ellie's decision seemed to be solidifying, her expression becoming more determined.

'Good idea, and you can send our love to him and Dani,' Whitney said, her smile broadening.

'I will,' Ellie responded, a grin tugging at her lips, the prospect of a holiday bringing a lightness to her demeanour.

George's phone pinged. She glanced down. It was a message from Sebastian Clifford, the ex-police officer, turned private investigator, who they'd worked with in the past. She read the message and frowned.

'What is it? Not bad news about the wedding,' Whitney asked.

'No, it's from Sebastian Clifford.'

'Seb? I didn't know you were in contact with him.'

'Yes, I agreed to speak to his daughter about possibly choosing to study forensic psychology at uni—'

'What?' Whitney spluttered. 'Since when has Seb got a daughter?'

'I didn't ask. He contacted me a while ago and asked if I'd meet with her and I agreed. He's suggested a date, but it's next week and I'm not sure I have the time to fit it in. I'll suggest after the wedding.'

'And you didn't for one moment wonder about this mysterious child?'

'I suppose it did come as a surprise, but I didn't ask questions.'

'Why didn't you tell me?'

'It slipped my mind.'

'Typical. The one time you actually come across something interesting, you forget to mention it. Well, I want to know more. Make sure you tell me when you're meeting them both, because I want to come with you.'

'I'm not sure that's appropriate,' George said, shaking her head.

'Why not? Seb and I are friends. You can speak to this daughter of his whilst we catch up.'

'I'll have to ask him first.'

'You're right, you will. I can't believe it. Seb with a daughter old enough to talk careers with you. He's only your age, isn't he? Can you imagine being the mother of a child that age?'

'I can't imagine being the mother of a child of any age, as you very well know.'

'Sorry. Have you and Ross talked further about it?'

'No. We're too busy focusing on the wedding to discuss that.'

'Whatever you decide, I'm sure he'll go along with. He loves you too much not to.' Whitney picked up her glass and downed her drink in one. 'I need another after the news you've given me. Would you like another?'

'No thanks, I promised Ross I wouldn't be late.'

'Actually, I should be getting back, too. Are you still on for a quiet hen party on Wednesday evening? You, me and Tiffany. Your last fling as a single woman.'

'I'd hardly call it a fling.'

'It's a joke, George. I knew you wouldn't want a rowdy night with a male stripper. This will be a fun evening with your best friends.'

'Thank you. It sounds perfect.'

EPILOGUE

Saturday, 23 March

A lump formed in Whitney's throat as she stared at the reflection of George in the mirror. Transformed and radiant, George in her wedding dress was the epitome of bridal beauty, her expression a mix of excitement and nervousness. Whitney had never seen her friend quite like it.

'What is it?' George asked, catching the questioning look in Whitney's eyes.

'You're so beautiful in that dress. I can't believe how stunning you are,' Whitney managed to say, her voice choked with emotion and her eyes brimming with tears of happiness. The bond they shared as friends and colleagues had only strengthened over the years, and seeing George in this moment was truly overwhelming.

'I must admit to being pleased with how the dress looks,' George replied in her usual nonplussed way.

Whitney smiled to herself. 'That comment is so like you. Well, let me tell you, being *pleased* doesn't come anywhere close.'

There was a knock at the door, and Whitney exchanged a glance with George, who nodded for her to open it.

'Yes?' she said, opening the door to a woman who looked to be in her late sixties, wearing a rose pink dress and matching bolero. In her hair was a fascinator.

'I'm Ross's mum, Aileen,' the woman said with a southern Irish accent. Her lips turned up into a warm smile. 'I thought George might like a glass of something.' She extended a glass of champagne.

'Come in,' Whitney said, stepping aside. George's soon-to-be mother-in-law looked as proud as any mother could be on her daughter's wedding day, and they weren't even related.

'Would you like a drink, George?' Whitney offered.

'Oh, no, I'd rather not, thank you,' George said, waving her hand dismissively, her mind clearly elsewhere.

'What about you?' Aileen enquired, looking towards Whitney.

Whitney wanted to stay clear-headed for George's big day. 'I'm fine, too, thanks,' she replied with a polite smile. 'I'm Whitney... the bridesmaid,' she added.

'We don't have time to talk whilst we're getting ready,' George said, her voice firm, conveying the need for privacy.

'Sorry,' Whitney added, aiming to smooth any ruffled feathers, hoping not to offend George's mother-in-law. 'I think she's got wedding nerves.'

Whitney wasn't at all sure that was the case, but she didn't know how well the woman knew George and her penchant for plain speaking.

'I totally understand,' Aileen said with an understanding tone. 'I have to tell you, George, you look pretty as a picture. Our Ross is going to be bowled over when he sees you.'

'Thank you, Aileen,' George said, her voice steady.

'Sorry to push you out of here, but I think the bride wants to be on her own... just the two of us,' Whitney said, gently ushering Aileen out of the room.

Whitney wanted to give George a moment of peace before the whirlwind of the wedding began, even if her friend didn't think she needed it.

'I'll see you soon, love,' Aileen said to George. 'My Ross is a very lucky boy.'

As the door closed behind Aileen, Whitney turned to her friend, her heart swelling with pride and love. 'This is your day, George. You're going to be an absolutely stunning bride.'

George smiled, the mix of nervousness and excitement in her eyes now tempered by the comfort of Whitney's presence. 'Thanks, Whitney. I can't believe this is actually happening. Am I doing the right thing? I've never been like other people. Being married hadn't even entered my head until Ross asked.'

'So what? It was because you hadn't met the right person. You deserve all the happiness in the world. Remember to breathe and take it all in. Today's going to be perfect.'

George nodded, her resolve visibly firming. 'I'm ready. Let's do this.'

Together, they shared a moment of quiet anticipation, both aware that the day ahead would be filled with joy, laughter, and memories to last a lifetime. Whitney couldn't have been happier for her friend and colleague on her wedding day.

* * *

A LETTER FROM THE AUTHOR

Dear reader,

Huge thanks for reading *Death's Shadow*. I hope you were hooked on the Cavendish and Walker series. If you want to join other readers in hearing all about my new books, you can sign up here:

www.stormpublishing.co/sally-rigby

If you enjoyed this book and could spare a few moments to leave a review that would be hugely appreciated. Even a short review can make all the difference in encouraging a reader to discover my books for the first time. Thank you so much!

If you'd like to learn more about my writing, receive a free novella and exclusive bonus content:

www.sallyrigby.com

Thanks again for being part of this amazing journey with me and I hope you'll stay in touch—I have so many more stories and ideas to entertain you with!

Sally Rigby

facebook.com/Sally-Rigby-131414630527848
instagram.com/sally.rigby.author

Printed in Great Britain
by Amazon